# EVE OF CHAOS

## DESTINY PARAMORTALS, #3

## LIVIA QUINN

### *Praise for Destiny Paramortals*

"My new favorite series!" "Okay, I'm hooked, Give me, give me some
more!!!" "A bit of magic, a lot of fun and a budding romance!"
"Tempest Pomeroy is the best new paranormal heroine of the year!"
"OMG, I loved this book. Run don't walk to the buy button." "Destiny. .
.is like a mini-vacation from the real world."

If you love Darynda Jones, Eve Langlais or Kristen Painter, you'll like
Livia Quinn.

BOOKS BY LIVIA QUINN

The Destiny Paramortals

Storm Crazy, #1

Cry Me a River, #2

Eve of Chaos, #3

Blame It on the Moon, #4

Take These Broken Wings. #5

Blood Moon #6

Blood Opal

Undone

Men of Honor (Contemporary Romance/Military)

Ridge

Luc

Nick

All I Want for Christmas

Men of Honor Box set

Sign up for Livia's spam-free newsletter to receive news and
exclusive offers. Click here to sign up

## Author's Note

As a music lover and professional singer, it's only natural that music would inspire me and my characters. Conor, my Scottish black dragon, surprised me by turned out to be a rock lover. I hope you enjoy getting to know Montana and Conor as things *heat* up in Destiny.

Sign up for my spam free newsletter to get my news and to be included in exclusive giveaways. Follow me on Bookbub and Amazon

As they say in my favorite escape, Britain . . .
*Caide Mile Failte',* A hundred thousand welcomes.
*Livia*
liviaquinn.com

*WELCOME TO DESTINY, HOME TO THE PARAMORTALS since...well, forever... where human neighbors and their new sheriff live alongside shifters, dragons, vampires and a family of djinn. . . Just don't tell the humans.*

A seer predicts that Dinnschencha warrior Montana will meet a dark, dangerous stranger at the Mardi Gras ball and in walks Dark Knight Conor de Sept Flambé. With his gleaming muscles, dragon-scale tattoos, and magnificent flashing swords, this clan leader fulfilled his destiny when he traveled through centuries to claim his fated mate and ensure the Paramortals' survival.

As Chaos—twenty-four hours when many Paramortals lose their power—fast approaches, Conor offers to prepare multi-shifter Montana for battle. Ready to fight for her family and town, nothing can prepare her for a war of the heart with a sexy dragon shifter who possesses an affinity for rock music and wants to show her his moves. *Yeah, right.* Sure, they can dance the night away, but their flames of desire threaten to scorch everything in sight. On the Eve of Chaos, as their passion burns, who will be left standing to fight?

A human sheriff, a dragon and a Dinnshencha warrior. Will it be enough to ward off the Paramortals' destruction?

*Fans of the Destiny Paramortals say:*

*"This is my new favorite series!" "WOW...just wow! Give me,*

1

give me some more." "OMG I loved this book. Run don't walk to the buy button!!" "It's like a mini-vacation away from the real world." If you like Darynda Jones, Eve Langlais or Kristen Painter, try Livia Quinn.

# PROLOGUE

*Saturday, before daylight*

"*Aw,* little dragon, do you think to scare me with your faux power? You forget, I know your kind."

What *kind,* Montana wondered. Dragons or Dinnshenchas? The enormous putrid smelling beast moved toward her. One foot slammed the thick Cypress floor making the house shudder, the next one coming down with a muffled thud followed by the sound of bones crunching, which went through Montana as if the woman on the other side of the room were her blood relative. She might as well be. The troll's victim moaned. *Thanks be to the goddess.* She wasn't dead.

The giant's malformed head cocked when his eyes locked on Montana, if you could call those twin pulsating orange bulbs eyes. They looked like they might drip or spew lava any second. More words came from its misshapen lips, "Why don't you try breathing fire, imposter?"

Montana faced the monster that had pounded his defense-less victim nearly to death. She lay near his feet, unmoving.

When the woman had called Montana asking for help, she hadn't said her abuser was a Dark Fae. She'd merely said, "I'm a dead woman if you don't get here soon." Now, its ugly twisted body, jagged fangs and growing magic threatened Montana as well. Running through the short list of beings that might catch him off guard she'd shifted, hoping the dragon form she chose would be strong enough to subdue, if not eliminate him.

Montana's Dinnshencha nature made it possible to shift into any form to defend a victim of abuse. She didn't know what dictionary the gods used in determining abuse, but she had her own, and if her Dinnshencha power didn't respond, her warrior nature was more than capable of taking care of the situation without resorting to any of her *Big Bads*.

But today, for some reason, her dragon wasn't intimi-dating this giant bi-ped.

Montana had changed countless times over the centuries but this was different; something was missing. Fleetingly, she allowed her thoughts to wander to the Para-moon. Was that the problem? The troll sensed her difficulty and hissed, "Go on, mini dragon. Torch me."

Why did he keep referring to her as a small dragon? She

was twice as tall as him and he was the one who should be worried since she always took on the powers of her shifted form. She opened her mouth but he just looked at her, one brow lifted— if you could call that wormy looking thing over his eye a brow. While he waited, he pressed his other foot down on the woman's chest. A tortured groan filled the room.

"Well...?" the bulbous eyes bounced.

Montana concentrated hard and tendrils of gray smoke teased from her nostrils. Okay, she was starting to get worried now.

"That's what I thought," the gnarly-faced creature said. His eyes suddenly burned with hostility, the long needle-like incisors and tongue growing larger as the muscles in his body bunched, signaling his attack. He sprang. Then a hot *whoosh* of flame flashed across Montana's vision. She'd had no time to jump back. As soon as she opened her eyes she realized—*it was over*. A fatal flame had scorched the offending abuser down to his one remaining foot.

Montana and the woman were safe.

Scorch marks marred the floor where the being had stood seconds ago. *Death from above!* Pretty accurate aim. Everything had been annihilated in front of Montana except the woman on the floor and the troll's foot, which was propped on her chest. The victim's one good eye opened and stared at the charred paw inches in front of her. Then her eye drifted toward Montana and and rolled up in her head.

Montana sighed. "Did I do that?" she wondered aloud and looked down her snout at the still oozing tendrils of gray smoke. A deep rumbling—like a hundred Vikings in the great hall enjoying a good joke—came from the direction of the ceiling. She followed the scorch mark up the wall to a blanket of stars against a night sky, and gasped.

The most beautiful creature she'd ever seen towered over her... and the house... with the moons, Luna and Cache', as his artistic backdrop. He leaned against what was left of the roof, dragon smugness—a special kind of arrogance singular to dragons—adorning his features. Well, he had a right to be smug. He'd taken out half the roof and the variant in one fiery exhale, without harming her or the woman on the floor.

"*Oooh*, you're good," she acknowledged, giving him a slight bow. She couldn't find it in her heart to complain about the remaining butt-ugly appendage even though it was probably obstructing the woman's breathing.

He was darker than the night, like a dragon shaped black hole except for his red rimmed snout, eyes and lips which shown like the reflector tape on the emergency vehicles she drove.

"Lassie, you dinnae ken the half o' it. Tell me. What made ye think ye could take on that *hackit* Faerie by yerself in yer lovely wee fog drakon form?"

At least he had a sense of humor. *Hackit* meant *really* ugly. Montana thought about what he'd said. Fog. *Hmm.* "So that's why I couldn't produce the fire..." she said, more to herself. He took her measure intently, his eyes traveling over her lithe ten-foot dragon form. When she changed back to her Valkyrie sized naked warrior body, she thought he smiled.

She stood perfectly still, innately comfortable in her nakedness. A small stream of fire sizzled from his nostrils and the irises swirled in his glowing red-rimmed eyes. His head disappeared from view and Montana felt a pang of disappointment, but he returned with two tiny scraps of fabric. Well, they looked tiny in his massive jaws. He opened his mouth just enough to allow the material to float down and land at her feet. She recognized it—her lingerie. You never knew where they were going to end up when you shifted.

His eyes drifted down lazily, the horny forehead wrinkled as he said, "I know yer secret, Victoria." Who would have thought a forty-foot dragon with a head the size of a house could wink *or* raise a non-existent brow? "Better cover yourself, Lassie. The coppers have arrived."

MONTANA BENT OVER TO PICK UP THE UNDERWEAR AND heard him laugh. The sound was like the rumbling of distant thunder and she felt excitement shoot along her nerve endings and heat the blood in her veins. She glanced toward the window as the sound of sirens came closer, and groaned. How was she supposed to explain this? When she looked up, he was gone. Typical male.

Even if Jack Lang responded, no, especially if Jack Lang responded she needed to have the blood and gore and troll pieces cleaned up, and she had to get out of there. She remembered their little tiff at the Mardi Gras ball when she'd told him she didn't need law enforcement interference. *Whoo boy*, she'd thought he was going to challenge her right there. That had been curious coming from the human sheriff. Challenge her how? It must have been his inner Navy commander coming out.

Problem was… Montana looked around. There was no way out except through the front door and that wasn't happening. She wasn't dressed to escape, and she'd be confronted by cops directly if she tried. Which of her *big uglies* could dispose of the fetid oozing foot. Damn that dragon anyway. He could have easily taken care of that. For a fraction of a second, she allowed herself a forbidden, covetous thought as to how he'd escaped. Had he lifted those wings, wings that could have spanned the block, graceful and powerful—*stop, Montana*. Just because she couldn't shift into anything that could actually fly… He had, of course, merely changed into a man and walked away. Or slinked off like the ungentlemanly coward he was.

Hoping the form she'd chosen would work because she could feel the gradual lessening of power as she shifted into the perfect scavenger, one that could make quick work of the appendage—a twelve-foot alligator. "Where is Lancelot when you need him?" she muttered through gator gums, as she angled her long snout sideways and snagged the foot with her teeth.

She almost gagged as the first taste of the troll's flesh hit her, or, the gator's tongue. "Arrgh." The sirens were getting louder so she forced it down with massive gulps, then she took a second to assess the woman's condition. The gator's stomach roiled and she belched. Time had almost run out on her before the cops arrived. How could that dragon have left her in this position, with an ogre's bloody foot the size of a pig to get rid of? If she ever saw him again, she'd make him pay.

Tires crunched on the turnoff to the house and the sound of sirens and voices outside told her help had arrived. She changed once again, but she'd miscalculated. The approaching eclipse was already having an effect. Her changes were less fluid, and this time she'd nearly gotten stuck halfway between the gator's body and her current choice, a mouse, which would make escape easier. After several agonizing seconds she completed the change and reminded herself if she got out of this predicament and was able to return to her human form, she would not shift again until after the Para-moon.

She planned to dart out when the EMTs entered but that didn't happen because Sheriff Lang entered, gun drawn, and shut the door behind him. Surely he wouldn't shoot a defenseless little mouse.

She turned her hair white to look more like a family pet... and burped. *Damn.*

Jack must have heard a squeak because he turned. She darted away, slamming headfirst into a wall, after seeing what she thought was a crack between the floor and the base board. Hadn't she heard that a mouse could skinny through a hole the size of a ball point pen opening? *Not.*

Montana wasn't used to being on the prey end of the predator spectrum. If she hadn't turned into the smallest animal on the planet, she wouldn't be looking like an idiot, bumping frantically into every possible obstruction. It made her appreciate the courage it took for her women to face the bastards in their lives, most of whom were bigger and stronger than them.

With that thought she stopped in the middle of the floor and stood— a teeny white mouse with the soul of a Dinnshencha— and faced the sheriff straight on, her mouse's tiny cobalt eyes locked on his pretty green ones. *Even a mouse can appreciate a man as good-looking as Jack.*

His head tilted, and his eyes narrowed momentarily, then he holstered his gun and said, "I've heard mice are smart, so when I open this door why don't you take a hike before someone steps on you."

For a scant second, she wondered if he'd recognized her. *Come on, Montana. Really?*

With her back feet spread wide, her upper body turned with his movement toward the door. As soon as he opened it, she scampered over the threshold and took off into the woods.

Her last view when she glanced back over her sleek furry shoulder was of Jack Lang standing back for the EMTs to attend the victim, a pair of red panties dangling from his pinky.

# CHAPTER 1

"Saved by the door buzzer", Tempe muttered as she picked her way across someone's lawn in her bare feet. That's probably what Jack had thought after a night of friggin' freaky lovemaking with her. He hadn't had to make excuses not to see her again, hadn't needed to lie to her, simply let things play out afterward.

Tempe stooped, gathered the layers of gray and peach colored tulle into her arms and made her way down the last block to Montana's house.

It was an odd structure for Louisiana, a tan stuccoed rambler with a broad concrete porch across the front. The house was split into four large rooms, with terra cotta floors and odd artifacts from the past on the walls. Montana's style was simple and bold, like her. No frills, no Feng shui. No sign of the opposite sex, or pictures of past relationships. If there was one thing you could count on, one *person* Tempe could count on to be the same, day after day, it was Montana.

Yesterday had started out with such promise. River was safe and she'd had a date to the Mardi Gras ball with Jack Lang, the sheriff of Destiny, her first ever invitation to a dance. Jack had arrived at Harmony Plantation last night in a silver stretch limo with his ex-wingman and deputy playing chauffeur. They'd returned to Jack's. She'd felt like Cinderella—until the pumpkin pulp hit the fan.

If anyone passed her right now, they'd undoubtedly see a lovesick expression on her face. Last night, Tempe had been afraid of what would happen if she lost herself in pleasure; she'd been worried he would think her a freak and unsure if she could control her power in such an intimate situation. She'd wanted to be *normal*, for him. But for once, Jack had been the one to push *her* to let go, gently prodding her and enjoying the magic as it unfolded. It *really was* magical, indescribable, and the last time was ramping up to be off the charts, when the door buzzer rang. And rang.

One doesn't just ignore a persistent doorbell in the middle of the night, especially not the parent of a teenager. Instead of the expected teenage drama though, standing on Jack's doorstep was someone Tempe'd hoped never to meet—his voluptuous (read that: trampy) ex-wife.

She'd thrown her arms around Jack as if she had no

doubt he would take her in and let her "spend time with her baby". Tempe wasn't sure if she'd been referring to Jordie or Jack. Jack didn't seem to like his ex much, but it was too early in their relationship for Tempe to predict what he would do. Men could be fickle. He hadn't exactly turned the woman away, and hadn't noticed— being all smooshed up next to her—when Tempe simply got dressed and let herself out the back door.

Talk about highs and lows. Was it any wonder she would turn to her calm, composed, self-possessed friend, Montana. Without those qualities, in her line of work, she'd go willy-nilly through the male population of Destiny annihilating each of them on their inevitable bad days. Montana and Dylan had been her closest friends for years, but after what happened recently, the relationship with Dylan was a big question mark.

Tempe walked across the patio to the rustic front door. The place must have been built to accommodate giants, with an arched entry almost as big as a castle's. With her hand raised mid-knock, *menori*, Tempe's inner storm perked up as a thump sounded against the door from the inside, followed by, "I've got you this time." Montana's voice.

Then the deep rumble of a male voice, "Not for long, lassie. Attack." Then, a clash of metal sliding against metal. Swords! Several strokes and parries could be heard as the opponents bumped against the walls. A chair toppled and Tempe thought a lamp fell over, but it didn't stop the momentum of the fight. Was Montana being threatened, or was she a willing participant? Surely, not in her own living room. Still, she did like her warrior arts…

*Menori* bristled, ready to unlock Montana's door, preparing to fight. Her energy sped through Tempe's veins and pushed power to the water and air filled cells of her body, but the results were sluggish.

A clank, followed by another sliding rasp of metal, and then the obvious indication that Tempe was intruding, "You have the most beautiful breasts." The heavy Scottish accent gave a clue as to Montana's *guest*.

Montana's throaty laugh filtered through the walls easily. "Maybe I'll allow you to pleasure them someday, warrior."

Tempe's eyes flew open. Montana not only had male company but was engaging in some kinky sword-fighting foreplay. At least that's what all the sighing and rhythmic wall banging usually meant. She'd never known Montana to hook up with a man, even assuming she might not "do" men. That gave her another little jolt, followed immediately by guilt. There was no one she'd rather see take "the fall" than Montana, *Ms. What-do-I-need-man-for, Dinnshencha.*

Tempe smiled. *You go for it, my friend.* If anyone deserved a special man in her life, it was Montana who championed women with no concern for the cost to her own personal life. She didn't think it was a conscious decision Montana made, just a product of her nature. Tempe turned away from the door, to allow *menori* some distance, and Montana her privacy.

TEMPE WAS TIRED OF BEING LET DOWN, TIME AFTER TIME. At a young age, with their father "dead" and their mother seemingly disinterested, Tempe had learned to rely on no one but herself for River's care. Then River had gone missing and she met Jack. He'd opened his door to sign for a package, and when their fingers met, something indescribable happened. Not to mention, there'd been all that tanned muscled glory, the water droplets from his hair and that little dollop of shaving cream trailing down his broad chest…

Jack, who had come to Destiny thinking he'd found a plain ol' Mayberry-ish small town to bring up his daughter, had surprised them all. From the time he'd seen Tempe unlock car doors with just a look, to his witnessing the full fury of her volcanic thunderstorm (he'd called it "beast mode"), he'd somehow managed to come to terms with Destiny's secrets and the existence of all kinds of creatures with intelligence. POPS, he called them— people of power.

She'd honestly expected him to take off but instead, he'd had nothing but praise for the community's support for their own and for his teenager, Jordie, their newest basketball star. His newfound acceptance of the *extra*-normal in Destiny had been put to the test last night though, when he'd overheard Aurora say that Jordie was a budding Paramortal. That was like saying, *Welcome to your worst nightmare, Jack* but he'd even reconciled himself to that after Tempe compared Paramortals to being in the military and defending the weak like he'd done his entire life. He was such an alpha hero.

They'd spent three memorable hours together, making love and, Tempe thought, building a foundation of trust. He'd not only taken the bizarre occurrences in his bedroom in stride but seemed to get a kick out of the whole experience. Then her coach had turned into a pumpkin. It just took a little longer than expected.

Wandering back down the lane from Montana's, she wondered what had transpired after she left Jack's. Jordie was at her grandparents' so if Georgeanne had been able to entice Jack back into his bed... *no,* she wasn't going there. Making sure she had the hem of the gown scooped up off the pavement, she started walking.

*What the—* and wound up at Dylan's.

# CHAPTER 2

THAT'S WHAT FEELING SORRY FOR YOURSELF AND NOT watching where you're going will land you—at your ex-lover's house where you lived until two years ago, when you caught him, to use an over-used cliché, "in the arms of another".

*You know more now,* she reminded herself.

*It doesn't make me like it any better,* she told herself's self. The bottom line was, they had baggage. Still they always seemed to cycle back to each other at work, as friends… and… no one could cheer her up quite like Dylan.

She looked at the well-maintained cottage. Painted a pale gray with burgundy trim, it was a small dwelling but with high ceilings that could accommodate Dylan's eight-foot Finrir. The flowers she'd planted when she lived with him had not been replaced. A ten-speed bike leaned against the front wall of the porch, but the garage was closed so there was no way to tell if he was inside. She walked up the steps to the door.

The reasons for his actions had been complicated and not entirely his fault. He'd been appointed her guardian until she went through the quickening. He'd apologized for hurting her, all of them had. Her friend, and mentor, Aurora, had been in on the secret of her father's non-death, as had all the Paramortals, bound by some plan that would supposedly keep her and River safe until her quickening. *Great plan.* River had been kidnapped and everything had changed.

Tempe knocked on Dylan's door. "Dylan." What was she going to say? What would he think? She pushed the buzzer and listened. He wasn't home. Dylan's bike practically shouted to her sore feet, "Take me!" and eyeing a roll of pink flagging on the air conditioner she made her decision. She wound the stretchy plastic around her waist, corralled the fluffy fabric and tied it out of her way. Gingerly placing her bare feet on the pedals she took off, pulling out her cell phone. Sometimes you were drawn to old habits even though you knew it wasn't the best path. If he turned that charm on her tonight, what would she do? Was there any spark left? *Tempe, you're pathetic.*

After what had happened at Jack's, she wasn't herself. She knew it, but she still dialed Dylan's number. It went straight to voice mail. Montana had company—that still blew her away—and Dylan was *Zeus only knew* where.

Wait! Why hadn't she thought of Kat, her mysterious friend, who worked nights from home and slept during the day. Kat lived at the edge of the swamp, in a refitted out-of-service hearse, of all things. She was a financial planner and also worked for the newspaper as an archivist. Nighttime suited her since she was a shifter, a huge black cat, like a puma or panther. Tempe'd never asked because Katerina was *protective* of her past, but she'd seen the cat a few times.

The hearse was limited on space, but Kat didn't need a lot of room for her wardrobe since everything she wore was black, black glasses (even at night), a black trench coat, black gloves and under it all what looked like a black, no kidding, cat suit. Jack called her 003. He thought she was on the run from somewhere or someone. Tempe just hoped Kat wouldn't mind some company. She hadn't actually visited her hearse before.

She reached into the bodice of the gown for her cell phone and steering the bike with one hand, dialed Dylan's number, once again getting his voicemail. Trying to maintain her balance and waiting too long to get her thoughts together cost her a chance at leaving a message.

Should she call back? What would she say? *I know it's early but I just wanted you to be the first to know, Jack's ex showed up and it looks like it's over.* Right.

Remembering her early morning coffee with Arabella the day before she mentally composed a new message. *I wanted to talk to you about something Arabella and I... sensed at the swamp yesterday morning. Oh, and there's this new guy in town I wondered if you knew anything about. And by the way, I stole your bike since Jack's ex showed up, and I was on foot.*

She decided a simple message would be much better. *Call me.* As she arrived at Kat's, the bike's front tire twisted on a loose rock and her foot slipped off the pedal. She grabbed the handle with the phone in her hand, and accidentally re-dialed.

Two things happened at once. She spotted the familiar SUV parked just beyond the former funeral transport, and someone's cell phone started ringing inside Kat's home. *Zeus' stray bolts!* She had to get out of there.

Before she could turn the bike around and emulate a streak of lightning leaving the campground, the rear door of Kat's "home" opened and Dylan's long lanky frame unfolded out of the boxy black hearse. He tucked his shirt into his pants, zipped up, and ran his fingers through his tousled black hair.

Tempe didn't think she'd ever seen Dylan look *tousled.* He was followed by the dark clad figure of Katerina. Tempe shook herself out of her shocked stupor and ended the call. Dylan peered at his phone, read the caller ID, and slipped his phone back in his pocket. Then he took Kat's hand and pulled her to him.

Moonlight illuminated them as their kiss grew more intimate. Tempe didn't dare move an eyelash. They might hear her—*or not*—they were pretty wrapped up in each other. If she didn't move or clear her throat or something, they would eventually discover her standing there, watching them.

There was no help for it. Dylan caught sight of her over Katerina's head. He was good. Kat may have felt him stiffen, but to Tempe he appeared unaffected, as if he was caught in his lover's arms every day. Well, hel*lo*, he was! By Tempe, at least.

"Tempe," he said, setting Katerina away from him.

Tempe heard a disgruntled snarl. *Oops.* "Uh, I... sorry, I'll just go now," she said, and dismounting the bike on one side, turned the handlebars away from the hearse. Dylan made a sound, and she looked back over her shoulder just in time to see Kat in her black puma form rise onto her back legs and take a swipe at Dylan with one large paw, claws fully extended.

Dylan dodged it, luckily for him, and shouted, "What—"

Tempe yelled, "Kat!" to distract her from pouncing on Dylan, which looked like her intent. She turned a hot golden glare on Tempe, and with a roar, leaped over Dylan's six foot four inches and disappeared toward Lightning Bayou.

Tempe shrugged, "Sorry. Was that your first fight? I guess I should have called first."

Dylan had been watching Kat's path toward the bayou, but now turned his narrowed gaze on Tempe.

Something niggled at Tempe's memory as Dylan walked

toward her, something about Kat's appearance. As the cat sailed over Dylan's head, a feature that hadn't been part of Kat's nature before was captured by the moon's rays—a full lion's mane.

# CHAPTER 3

"After the ball was over... Sweetheart my love, my own..." Montana's raspy alto crooned as she twirled from one object to another in the large great room. The place was a shambles, chairs overturned, her ancient displays catty-wumpus on the walls, cushions everywhere, and wine glasses on their sides by the couch.

If she were human she might have said it was the wine that started it all...

She'd *had* several glasses of wine before Elder Rawlins announced *him* at the ball the night before. Seeing him, she'd been enamored, wasted, mesmerized, *in heat.* From the tips of those beautiful and deadly swords to the armored shoes, not to ignore the fine muscles, the black silk of his luscious hair falling to his shoulders, nearly covering the winged tattoos... she'd wanted him.

She hadn't *wanted* to want him. If she hadn't known better she might have described herself as a bitch in heat. Everyone else, every thing else—the music, the food, her friends—all of it had faded away. She'd been locked on the Dark Knight, as if the huge ballroom was empty—the ball, their own private affair.

Montana ran his name across her lips, "Conor de Sept Flambé... the Knight Flambé... Conor." Montana was not a woman who experienced shyness or false modesty, and especially not guilt over her instant attraction to any being. It was instinct—what Tempe or the humans would call hormones, but hormones weren't an issue for Dinnshenchas. They didn't exist, and would quite get in the way of one's tasks.

Now desire... that was a whole other animal. The Knight pinged her desire like a proverbial arrow through the heart. Who's arrow—Cupid's? *Oh, no, not going there.* This was lust, pure and simple, and half of it was for the damn swords.

She'd been unable to break the compulsion to track him wherever he went. At the bar, a short curly headed blonde in a purple Maid Marian costume had flirted shamelessly, relentlessly, trying to draw him into conversation. With her baby-blues locked on him, her hands had fluttered up to illustrate her words, but his dark head turned and his black eyes sought out Montana's, and held. There was no question in them, no suggestion, no feigned interest. It was a look that said, *I'm putting up with these inane humans, but I'm here for you—just say the word.*

Her eyes had flared sending one eyebrow arching up, as she swallowed. Had he spoken to her telepathically or was her warrior soul hearing his? She didn't know. She was definitely intrigued though. She realized if it hadn't been for him she would have left by now, having only attended anyway for the charity, which was important enough, critical enough to the lives of her families, that she put up with women like Jane and irritating males like Dick. Right now she felt the distinctive urge to twist one curly blonde's head around and point her in the direction of the young redheaded Pirate across the room who couldn't seem to take his eyes off her.

Instead, the little ninny was trying to gain the affections of the Knight Flambé.

*Go away, Sweetie.* He's a thousand times more man than you could handle, she'd thought. Then the inexplicable happened. He bent over, those large metal-cuffed hands coming down delicately (so gently Montana groaned) on the short blonde's shoulders. His head bent slowly toward hers—no! *Surely, not.* Montana punched out a breath she hadn't realized she was holding and almost transformed into D-mode—when he suddenly turned the young woman, pointed at the redheaded man, and whispered in her ear.

The girl's eyes widened when Blackbeard, well, Redbeard broke into a smile, beaming on her like sunshine. The Knight gave her a gentle shove as if launching a boat away from the shore, the momentum sending her floating across the floor, like a dingy in the pirate's fleet as she drifted toward the mother ship. When she arrived, he took her hand, brought the *little boat* into port, linked her arm over his and led her away, out of everyone's view. She'd never even looked back.

Montana had felt the Knight's gaze on her then. She met it, wondering—had he merely suggested or enlightened the young woman about the interest of the auburn haired man, or had he hypnotized her? She raised a brow again in question. The corner of his mouth may have canted up just a tad. She saw the answering complimentary sparkle in his black eyes, as if saying, *She was just a child. You know she's not for me.*

Rare self-doubt had slithered down Montana's spine then and she'd turned away, walked to Aurora's table, and flopped down in the chair next to her. She'd been sipping soda with her wine all night for the indigestion that still lingered from eating that horrible troll's foot. She pushed the glass away and plopped her chin on her palm.

Sulking wasn't like her. She pretended, tried to be interested in anyone else in the room; even made a pretense of conversation with a couple of Aurora's customers, but her eyes traveled back faithlessly to the bar where a pair of black eyes behind an eerily organic looking mask tracked her movements like a raptor. She turned to find Aurora studying her. "What?"

Aurora's angled brow needed no real interpretation, but she confirmed it anyway, "Don't look at me, I warned you."

# CHAPTER 4

FOR THE REST OF THE EVENING, NO MATTER WHERE she was, if she turned her head, and looked across the expanse of revelers she'd find his eyes fastened on hers, as if he'd been waiting for her to turn. Once, she turned back toward the bar but it was oddly clear, only Flambé standing there, framed by the oak counter, one of his swords standing in front of him on its hilt, the tip nearly reaching the Knight's chest. He'd been cleaning it, shining and stroking the deadly edges with a cloth, so intimately acquainted with them that he wasn't even watching.

His attention was all on her, the rims of his eyes lined like a predator's, causing her to shiver briefly, but if that look was for her, he should know she was not prey. By her very nature, predators were her enemy. And still she felt the pull of pure heat as if they were connected in some way.

Sometime after Tempe and Jack left, the orchestra had suddenly stopped playing the zydeco music and the unlikely strains of a minuet had filled the room. Everyone looked up in surprise. Then as it had when he entered, the crowd split, giving the swordsman a wide berth as he strode purposefully across the ballroom floor toward Montana's side of the room, his gaze locked on hers the whole way. Surely... she broke the contact to search the area around her, but there was no one nearby. He was coming for her. Her Dinnshencha reared up, readying for this formal meeting. It seemed impossible that she hadn't actually met him yet.

His broad black tattooed shoulders led as his long strides moved closer, the flared pants hugging his powerful thighs, flowing around his calves, the swords catching the light overhead, making them flash with dazzling fire. He came to a stop inches from her and the air seemed to leave the room, the sounds of feet shifting, voices, and laughter dying as he planted his feet in front of her.

The crowd waited. She waited. Not a muscle, pore or eyelash flickered while the room held its collective breath in expectation. The Knight's arms rose, stretching the thick tattoos across his shoulders, giving the appearance of wings spreading, preparing to lift off.

The room inhaled as one. Flambé's eyes dropped; he brought one hand to his torso, and bowed. For a matter of seconds all she could see was his shiny black shoulder length hair and the leathery detail on the tattoos. The collective *"ahhs"* of the women in the room penetrated her awareness as he straightened again and spoke. "Lass, may I hav' this dance?"

DANCING WAS AS MUCH A PART OF A DINNSHENCHA AS her sword. So of course, she'd danced with him. And danced, and danced. If that's what you'd call their connection, their movements, his leading her while the music played that minuet. She'd never danced a minuet before in her long life, just another indication of how bedazzled she'd been.

The minuet ended, followed by a waltz as she stayed in his arms. She wasn't sure how that happened. So much about Conor fascinated her. The aura of danger, so like her own. His overwhelming strength. His secrets. And of course, the swords!

The beat changed to a rock song Montana recognized, Imagine Dragons' "Battle Cry".

"Did you request that song?" she asked him. His eyes behind the dark mask had sparkled and his lips widened in a grin to expose straight white teeth. *Of course, Montana, what did you expect? Fangs?*

He said, "I thought you might like that one. I didnae just shoot straight into the 21st century, ye ken? I lived through them all and each has its own music flavor." Okay, he'd finally surprised her.

"Right now my favorite tis Little Dragon." His lips had

tilted up in a smile as his eyes glinted oddly. She couldn't help herself, she'd smiled back.

The sighs of the women near her broke the spell and Montana frowned, his words striking a familiar chord. "Little dragon?"

The knight's eyes brightened behind the mask. "Yes, Victoria... my brave wee dragon."

MONTANA'S EYES HAD GONE WIDE, SHOULDERS RIGID, and if he hadn't held her wrists in his metal-clad iron grip, she'd have changed right there in the ballroom, in front of the humans. Her vision had gone red, then black tinged before she could see him again. He had the good sense to look wary.

"Let. Go." He had power. *No one* should have been able to keep her from shifting.

A heartbeat later she was striding toward the back garden, the cobalt silk flying around her. A couple sitting on the concrete bench in the center of the courtyard scampered when she strode down the walkway. She knew she was a formidable sight. She usually didn't get mad without changing. Right then, all that rage was bottled up with no where to go.

Heavy footsteps followed her into the outer yard and she heard the heavy doors close.

"Why are ye so mad, Victoria? When I saw you last—"

She whirled and it was a mark of his power that he didn't even flinch at the sight of her anger, or feel threatened. Well, of course! He wasn't just a Knight-man with fancy swords, he was an ancient *awesome* dragon. *Montana...* now was not the time to be admiring this smug creature.

She grit her teeth, "When last I saw you, you arrogant excuse for a savior, you left me locked in a house with the cops arriving, no way of disposing of that abuser's giant foot. You're not a Knight with any kind of honor, *methinks.*"

He blinked, and one black brow rose in an elegant arch. Montana thought he was smart enough to let her vent. He wasn't. "I knew *yooud* handle it." His accent seemed to get stronger when he let his guard down.

She'd nearly lost it. "How? How could you know I would handle it?"

He shrugged. "Warriors know." She'd sputtered and raged.

"You left me with diminishing power and no way to escape. I had to change into a friggin' mouse. *Goddess,* a mouse. I could have been stepped on, or worse. I almost got stuck mid-shift." *Why was she whining?*

"Ah." What did that mean? "I apologize. I haid to be gone me'self ye ken. Any longer and I would'nae have been unable to fly away unseen. I couldnae risk being seen in my man form yet, Victoria."

"Stop calling me that. My name is Montana. The name in my—" *Oh, gods, she was about to explain the brand name of her lingerie to a dragon.*

"Montana is no name for a warrior like you."

She'd gawked at him, "And Victoria is?"

"*Aye.* It means victorious." His eyes had flared with appreciation, and then he began to pace.

She stood there watching him because he was simply too fine not to. His long strides, even in such a small area, were so forceful, so decisive. This Knight— "Are you really a Knight?"

He spun. So fast her eyes didn't catch them his swords were out and crisscrossed in front of her head, one tip at either ear. Her eyes went wide. One quick flick of his wrists and she would be a headless Dinnshencha.

She narrowed her gaze on those dark eyes. "All *that* told me is that you're fast." Her eyes drifted down across his ridged abs, stopping just below his belt. His followed... to where a short-sword tip was introducing itself to his dragonly parts.

He gave her a nod and the swords withdrew. "Even with diminished power you are awesome, my wee dragon." He flipped the giant swords over his head and before she could move, they sheathed themselves behind his shoulders.

"Smooth," she breathed.

"Mayhap I can make up for my lack of manners. You will lose your Dinnshencha powers tomorrow. I could show you a few of my moves."

"Oh, that's a new one," Montana snickered, but when she looked at him, his gaze was thoughtful. He was entirely serious. "How do I know you can show me anything worth my tim—"

She felt the prick on her breast before she even saw him move. This time there'd been no chance to react. He'd been blindingly, invisibly fast. He must have been toying with her before. She looked down to see that he had made several slits in the ruffles of her dress, set one fine spaghetti strap free and barely nicked the skin between her breasts.

Then, eyes swirling like they had at the Bentsons', he whipped the mask off his head and leaned toward her, the silky black strands drifting over her chest as his tongue flicked out and licked the droplet from her skin. Heat scorched through her blood.

She'd gone hot and wet at the sight. "You were toying with me," she said, eyes narrowed.

"Merely measuring your strength. You didn't even realize when you went up against the *hackit* Fae that your strength was waning. It 'tis even less now. You must allow me to hone yer skills."

He'd said *you must*, but he'd made it sound like she had a choice. Would he walk away if she turned him down?

"Why are you here?"

"We shall discuss it later, *after* you let me instruct you in the deadly arts."

Well, what could a woman of war say to that? To a Dinnshencha, offering to "hone her skills" was better than sex. Well, almost.

Montana tamped down the thrill and tied one last time to reduce him to quivering apologies. "I had the worst case of indigestion after eating that thing's foot."

"I'll try to have better aim next time, eh?" was all he said as he'd offered his arm and led her back to the ball-room. He may have intimidated the men but the women sure as hell were drawn to him.

What if he was using some kind of strong glamour that affected even her? She'd have to watch herself.

She'd gone back to the dance floor with him because she loved to dance. He'd chosen a certain repertoire for the band and as other revelers kept to the edges of the floor, he taught Montana some new "dance moves" choreographed to everything from pop to heavy metal. He'd said using contemporary music gave a current exigency to the training. By the time they'd left to continue elsewhere, she knew his moves by heart.

# CHAPTER 5

TEMPE COULDN'T BEGIN TO KNOW WHAT DYLAN WAS thinking. His usual dark aura was the color of an overcast sky. Dylan could be very intimidating with his dark scowls and taciturn personality, but Tempe knew Dylan too well to be afraid of him.

"What are you doing here?" he asked. Stepping back to check the bike out, he raised those dark brows. "Stealing bikes now, are we?" He set his legs in a wide stance, then the subtleties of her appearance finally made it through his worries about Kat, and he placed both fists on his hips. "What happened? I thought you went to the ball. Where's Lang?" He glanced toward the entrance of the park as if expecting to see Jack drive up any minute.

Tempe didn't look at him but pretended to stare into the woods. "Probably with his ex-wife and daughter. You can pick up your bike at my house later," she said referring to Harmony Plantation, hers and River's money sucking monstrosity of a DIY home-remodeling project. She started to make the circle with the bike but his big strong hand locked onto her wrist, stopping her.

"Get off the bike," he said, in a firm voice but with none of his usual surliness.

She couldn't read his expression but he made it sound like it was her only option. She didn't have the energy to fight him. Tempe slipped off the seat and turned toward the road. He didn't let go, pulling her back around. "Come on, I'll give you a lift and you can tell me about it." She nodded but didn't look at him. She couldn't bear to see pity in his eyes. Or any hint of *I told you so.*

He opened his rear door and placed the bike inside. "Get in." Tempe rolled her eyes and pretended not to listen as she untied the makeshift rope from around her dress and let it fall in messy crinkled glory to the ground.

"You look beautiful, Tempe, even in bare feet, and that wrinkled dress," he said. "Pick it up."

She didn't know what to say. She wished their relationship were different, wished they had less baggage. Maybe one day.

"Where to? Back to Jack's?" That black brow lifted as if he wouldn't mind a challenge about now.

"You'd take me there, wouldn't you?" She smiled at him. "Why? Curiosity? Needing a good fight?"

Dylan studied her for several seconds. He shrugged and rolled his shoulders. He'd been more bothered by what had happened with Kat than he was letting on. Tempe asked, "What was going on back there, anyway? And since when does Katerina's lion *roar*? I thought all she could do was purr."

Dylan blew out a breath. "She wasn't..." he scratched his ear, "...herself tonight." Meaning, Dylan knew her well enough to compare against other nights? *Well.* How long had that been going on?

"I haven't noticed anything. She was fine..." when was that exactly... "the night Dutch followed me, and she seemed okay Friday when we stormed the cabin and rescued River."

"Since last night. Her moods have been erratic. I tried to get her to tell me what happened before she came to Destiny. You know she's hiding something... bad. In the middle of makin—um, afterwards, I looked over at her and I swear she was getting ready to bite me, and her fangs were shaped more like a vampire's. She wasn't so much offended at my questions, as defensive and then she clammed up on me. When the phone rang and she saw the caller ID, she... got upset."

He rubbed the back of his neck and sighed. "I don't know. Her power certainly didn't seem as if it's taken a hit since the Para-moon's approach. If anything, it seems like it increased." He slowed and pulled over near the bayou. "Have you noticed any changes in your power yet?"

"Well, it's so new, I'm not sure I could tell."

Dylan's eyes moved over her features, her hair, her eyes, "That won't be a problem, believe me."

"Kat's were-lion was different, the roar and… you didn't see her, Dylan. She looked like a full grown *male* lion, with a mane and everything."

Dylan's look was distant as his mind ticked off the possibilities. "That's not normal for Paramortals during the power down, not blooded ones anyway. It has to have something to do with her past."

"She just showed up here six months ago. Do we know she's a Paramortal?" Tempe asked.

Dylan was thoughtful. "Yes. Remember, Aurora settled that when she moved here last year under such mysterious circumstances. Maybe she's a mixed species."

That brought up a whole new set of questions for Aurora.

"When was the last Para-moon, Dylan? Aurora said they don't happen very often."

"It was roughly four hundred years ago. Aurora said this one would be different because of the 'aspects' and Luna's path and position. "We won't know exactly how it will affect each of us until the eclipse tonight. I suspect things could get a little dicey."

"Ya think? Jack's going to love that."

Dylan cocked his head to the side. "Tell me what happened with Jack. Didn't you two go to the Mardi

Gras ball? I heard you were seen in a silver limo driving away from Harmony." He raised an inquiring brow. "What went wrong?" That question came with a bit of a growl. Tempe couldn't help it. She got a little lift from the idea that Dylan would be a bit protective of her.

"Someone from his past showed up," she said. *"Zeus' blazing bolts."* She remembered what Aurora had predicted and grabbed Dylan's forearm. "That's what Aurora meant. The evil—"

"Huh? Go back to the beginning, Tempe."

"Okay, yes, Jack took me to the ball. It was great. Better than great. " She slapped her hands to her face and massaged her temples. *"Zeus,* I need to catch you up on everything that happened last night. Jane Fortune and Aurora were doing readings to raise money for Montana's charity, and Montana talked me into getting mine done. Aurora said I would encounter quote, 'evil from your lover's past'." Tempe paused to watch Dylan's reaction. Nothing. "I thought she meant you, but she was talking about Jack!"

Tempe swept her hands through her hair, sending it flying. "Jack and I were…" *well, this was awkward,* "…at his house when the front door bell went off. It went on and on, at 3:15 in the morning! We were afraid it might be an emergency with Jordie, so he answered it."

"Well, who was it?"

Tempe's eyebrow hiked as she looked at Dylan. "Jack's ex-wife, and *man-slayer* is too tame a word. She's the kind of woman every man thinks he wants, and then begs to be rid of in the end. Anyway, he seemed shocked to see her, but she threw her arms around him and said, 'Jackie, honey, I'm home'." Tempe parroted Georgeanne's words. "Let's just say, he didn't stop me from leaving."

Dylan frowned, "Mm, I don't know, Tempe. I'll admit to some jealousy, *undeserved* jealousy, when I first met Jack but this doesn't sound like him. Didn't he say one of the reasons he wanted to find a normal place to raise Jordie was because of his disastrous marriage? He got full custody, remember. I've come to respect that human in the short time he's been here. And there's Aurora's reading to consider. She referred to the woman from his past as 'an evil'. Maybe you should give him the benefit of the doubt when you see him. You said, 'everything that happened' at the ball. What else?"

"I don't know if this has to do with the Para-moon but Mr. Jackson and Inez Messer showed up together." Dylan's brows rose. "*Uh-huh*. And Jane Fortune and Dickhead are apparently keeping company all of a sudden, but put that aside, it's not the most important thing. Do you by any chance know a… Samurai Knight by the name of Conor de Sept Flambé?"

"A Samurai Knight?" His thick brows bunched. "Is there such a thing?"

Tempe threw up her hands, "I don't know but it was the way he was dressed. I don't know if that's what he is, but when he announced, Jack and Montana both reacted to him like they were fixin' to get it on. He had these two shiny jagged looking swords on his back and, like… bat wings or something tattooed across his shoulders. And man, was he buff!" Dylan coughed a laugh. "Well, I'm just calling a *Knight* a *spade*, and get this… Montana completely dismissed Aurora's prediction earlier that she was going to meet, and I quote, 'a dark dangerous stranger'."

"Hmm, Aurora's good," was all Dylan said.

"Is that all you have to say? What do you think he's doing here? Does it have something to do with Chaos? Could he be *Aretuu*?" Jack would simply ignore that term for their enemies and call them 'bad POPs'. It was actually a pretty appropriate nickname.

Dylan rubbed his chin, then shook his head. "My gut says, *not* Aretuu. Did he seem threatening? Did he try to manipulate anyone, question, confront or mingle?"

Tempe shook her head. "Not really. He just sort of… watched. Of course, Jack and I left early."

Dylan laughed, "Good for Jack."

"No, that wasn't the reason. We would have stayed until at least the midnight celebration but um, something else happened." Tempe took a deep breath. "Jack overheard Aurora telling me that Jordie is a new Paramortal. You might say he…"

"Freaked?" Dylan guessed eyebrows raised.

"A bit. He side-kicked the big oak tree outside the hall. It'll never be the same." She smiled.

"Well, he apparently got over it, right? I mean you two took the party to his place…"

"Yes, and it was quite a party."

Tempe couldn't strip the smile from her face even if it pained Dylan but he surprised her by saying, "You deserve good things, Tempe. And happiness. Hang in there until after Chaos and let's give Jack a chance. Besides, we're going to need him."

Tempe nodded. "What can one human do against our enemies, Dylan, if it gets bad?"

"He won't be alone. There will be others under the Oath who won't lose power, those who aren't blood bound. But this brings up a question, how did Jordie get to be a Paramortal? That would mean one of her parents is—"

"Yeah, well, Jack seems to think it's his bitchy wife —ex-wife."

"I see—" Dylan's words were cut short by a nightmarish roar from deep in the bayou. The sound pierced the quiet Sunday morning, silencing nature, causing *menori* to stir and eliciting a growl from Dylan.

When it ended, Tempe said, "That wasn't Kat, was it?" Dylan's form wavered. "Dylan. Can you change?"

He grimaced. She had her answer. "I'm going to drop you at Harmony and check that out."

Tempe shook her head. "No, just let me borrow your bike. I want to go by Montana's. And *this* could be important. Bella and I were sitting by the Forge yesterday morning and sensed something, a darkness, an evil presence. She said I should tell you about it. With everything that's happened, it slipped my mind."

Now was not the time to whine about him not telling her the full scope of his duties to the Paramortal community. She'd just found out that he wasn't only working as an investigator for the postal service, but also looking into some missing Fae, and who knew what else.

Dylan nodded, "It's okay. I'm here now. Let me do a little Finrir style investigating."

"Be careful, Dylan."

"Aww, you do care," he teased.

She started to slap him but another scream rent the morning and he said, "I'd better go. Come on, I'll get the bike out for you."

As Dylan drove off, Tempe tied her gown up again, and keeping her eyes on the shadowy woods and bayou, started pedaling toward Montana's. The conversation with Dylan had also reminded her that someone had to bring Jack up to speed today on what to expect during the next twenty-four hours.

By the time Tempe got back to Montana's she was

worried. Maybe she should have knocked earlier and made sure she was okay, but hey, Dinnshencha warrioress. She did feel a little like a stalker waiting outside until Montana's company left. While she waited, her mind traveled back doggedly to Jack. What was he doing? Had he given in and let his ex-wife stay? Had she tried to seduce him? Would she even have to?

*Come on, Temp, believe in yourself a bit, will you?* She remembered their lovemaking, the fireworks, the literal storm in their bed. And Jack hadn't seemed to be turned off. Even Dylan said to give him the benefit of the doubt. But *that* woman had had a powerful aura, unfortunately Tempe could only see it, not make sense it. What could she still do, she wondered. She commanded *menori* to scope out Montana's house, just a simple reconnaissance.

*Menori's* connection was weak though so Tempe recalled her, but she knew when *menori* returned that Montana's visitor was gone. She pulled the front door open, not worried about startling her friend with her acute senses. What she saw in Montana's living room set her on her heels.

# CHAPTER 6

"AFTER THE BALL WAS OVER... MY SWEETHEART MY LOVE, my own..." Montana's lovely alto filled the room.

*Zeus' lacy drawers!* Tempe gawked. Was this due to the approach of the Para-moon? Where was her friend Montana, the Amazon warrior? Things were getting weirder by the hour. Hadn't she used words earlier like restrained, dispassionate, unflappable, unemotional, to describe Montana, when the woman before her was downright... happy. Radiant, blissful, beaming, on cloud nine... those descriptions would be more accurate.

Still in the tiers of royal silk, her blue-black hair tumbled around her shoulders as she moved. Then Tempe realized Montana's steps weren't dream-like but precise, choreographed. She'd never seen Montana in a dress until last night, much less a backless one that exposed the blue Dinnshencha birth mark high on her left shoulder. She looked feminine, sexy. It wasn't that she usually looked masculine… more like the promise of deadly force. Whatever had brought about this change, it was of some consequence.

"After the ball—" Montana caught sight of her on the last spin. "Well, are you just going to stand out there and stare or come in and tell me why you've been roaming the streets all night?"

Tempe looked around the room. It was nine o'clock in the morning and there were wine glasses on the counter. The usually meticulous house showed signs of a party— sheets dragged from the bedroom and stretched across the floor in front of the fire— or a fight. A chair and stool were upended, the painting over the couch canted at an odd angle, the bed when she looked through the bedroom door, covered by only the bottom sheet.

"You… like to dance?" *Well, duh, Tempe.*

"Surprised?" Montana resumed her sliding, twirling and humming. She closed her eyes, extending her arms elegantly. "Dancing is how my people celebrate, although normally it's outside under the moon after a great battle."

"Well, don't let me stop you," Tempe said, grinning. "Tonight should make for some extraordinary moon dancing." Montana was definitely *not right* today, but then who was? The flush of her skin, the singing, the clever sparkle in her eyes instead of her normally cool inscrutable expression.

"You met someone," Tempe said but Montana ignored

her. She extended one leg and executed a perfect three-sixty on the other, making spirals with her arms.

Tempe walked around trying to see her face. "Hello. I'd like to speak to Montana. Whoever has taken over her body, please let her out."

"After the ball was over..." Montana started humming again, "my sweetheart, my Knight..."

Tempe paused. She'd been about to sit on the barstool when something caught her eye. She plucked a tooth-pick from the empty plate of cheese and raised a pair of lacy neon blue panties to Montana's eye level. "Hmm."

"Give me those," Montana growled, but the growl was at odds with the smile she couldn't seem to suppress. She waltzed into the kitchen and returned with two cups of coffee. Tempe saw what was surely the mark of a whisker burn on Montana's neck.

"The place is trashed." Tempe looked around at the disarray. "What did you do here, anyway? I thought I heard swords earlier. Don't get me wrong. If you're happy, I'm happy for you." Maybe Montana had midnight liaisons all the time. Tempe took a sip of her coffee, looked into the cup as if it held tea leaves and could divine answers.

"I had the best night of my life." Montana's deep blue irises bored into Tempe's. "Magnificent. Raging, and it's been a long life." She swooped down, grabbed the sheet and twirled letting it billow and flare with her spins.

Tempe couldn't get over the change in Montana. She'd been at the ball the night before. Montana had had no escort and as far as Tempe knew she didn't date.

This would all not seem so implausible if Montana were human, or any other type of non-human other than what she was. Tempe would have been less surprised if she'd found out she was asexual. With such a strong drive to protect women from abuse, it seemed Montana would have a life-long antipathy toward the opposite sex, at least in personal relationships. She and Rafe, her EMT partner, though, seemed to get along great. She was just realizing how much she didn't know about her friend.

"You sure are mellow."

"Shut up." While she watched Montana dance across the floor with that satisfied smile, Tempe ran back over the events of the night before...

The ball had been a grand pageant of gowns, costumes, food and music. Formal, invitation only, it had gone on late into the night. Aurora and Jane had been doing readings. There'd been the regular Krewe business, announcements, long boring introductions, and then...

"The Dark Knight!" Tempe turned wide eyes on Montana. She grinned like a Cheshire cat.

"*Zeus' blue nuggets*, Montana. You didn't."

"Oh, but I did," she said and her laughter sent her off

into more spins and slashes. "I learned more about fighting last night than I have in two hundred years." Her hands hit the chimes hanging from the ceiling between the kitchen and great room and she ran her fingers back and forth across them, making them jangle.

"So, you're saying what I heard was just... training?" Her voice rose indicating her skepticism.

Montana chuffed, "No. Not *merely*—it was lethal, battle tested, strategic sword fighting. That dra—Knight is a brilliant teacher. I've never seen a warrior move like he does." Montana was excited, her eyes a brilliant blue.

"And—"

"And... that's it." Montana's head tilted, peering over at Tempe. "It couldn't possibly beat your night." Montana frowned. "What did you do? Sleep on the ground in that gown? The dress-up police are going to have your head."

When Tempe's face fell, Montana stopped swaying.

*Oops*, Tempe had forgotten whom she was dealing with. She looked down at her dress and immediately wondered if she could keep this to herself. Then Montana's Dinnshencha kicked in, her eyes turning to ice blue frost. "What happened? Did someone hurt you?"

"No, well, not physically. I mean," Tempe sighed, "it's a long story."

"I'll kill him." The words were soft and deadly.

"No, no. It's nothing like that, exactly."

"Well, exactly *what* then?" Now she was all Dinchennsha, hands on her hips. The beautiful feminine dress no longer suited her demeanor. She was fearsome.

"Could I have a glass of water?" Tempe's voice came out in a high pitch. Maybe a diversion would back her down a tad. But after filling a used coffee cup with water and setting it on the counter with a little more force than necessary, sloshing liquid over the edge, Montana took a stance in exactly the same spot and said, "No stalling."

Tempe sighed and started talking. "Okay, you saw us leave—"

"Aurora told me. I assumed Jack was upset."

"Finding out your teenage daughter is about to become a freak of nature would tend to upset you, but by the time we got to his house," Montana's eyebrow rose, "he was asking questions and seemed to come to terms with it." Tempe grinned, "What followed was pretty spectacular. There were even fireworks, literally, in the bedroom, and he didn't panic. He was fine... until... um, his ex-wife showed up at the door."

A warning growl surged up from Montana's throat, her eyes taking on that frosty color again.

"Yeah, she threw her arms around him, while I stood there in his bathrobe, fresh from our lovemaking."

~

MONTANA COULD FEEL TEMPE'S HEART CRYING AS IF IT were her own. It was tough to maintain control once she got a whiff of any kind of wrong-doing aimed at a female, much less a dear friend. Her Dinnshencha was close to battle mode. "Why didn't he send her away?" Montana asked softly, through clenched teeth.

Tempe seemed put off by Montana's harsh reaction, "Okay, now, wait until I'm finished. I mean… she was a bitch, but it would have only made it worse for Jack—" Montana growled louder, "—if I'd stayed."

"Montana?" Tempe's voice held an odd emotion—fear?

"I need you to tell me what happened, Tempe." Montana actually thought her reaction had been pretty low key. The Para-moon was responsible for that. As she'd discovered the previous day at Mrs. Bentson's house, her power was rapidly diminishing. But if someone had hurt her friend—a certain sheriff someone —she was sure she'd have no trouble taking him out on her own. Even without her new moves.

A growl escaped before she could stuff it, and Tempe's eyes widened, sparkling like exploding stars. Thunder rumbled across the concrete floor of the living room… *Well, lookee here!* Montana clamped down on her Dinnshencha, before it could react to a perceived attack —from her friend's Tempestaerie, knowing as the more mature Paramortal, she might be the only one of them who could prevent disaster.

Paramortals couldn't fight each other could they, she wondered. Wouldn't the Oath prevent that? Had it just been a natural defensive instinct or was something else at work? Montana had been dancing on air (practicing, she told herself) when Tempe arrived and she'd missed her friend's disheveled condition. Now she *really* looked at her. There was barely any color in her dull red hair. The streaks were gone.

Tempe said, "I—I think she caught him off guard."

*Oh, the ex, right,* Montana thought. She paced to the wide window and looked out at the gray clouds moving low across the sky. Snow had begun to drift earthward.

Tempe threw up her hands, "I'm not sure what to do, Montana. What if—" Montana stepped toward Tempe carefully and when she didn't get any hostile vibes, she hugged her. "I've seen how that man looks at you, Tempe. Let's give him a chance to explain, but you know me, I have to keep tabs on the situation. I don't have a choice."

Tempe sighed deeply. "I know, but just check with me before you go lopping off his head or anything. Now the ex..." she smiled. "Have at it."

Montana grinned, wondering if she'd imagined the friction between them. "Sorry, I don't do women, even when they deserve it."

Tempe's chuckle was lighter as she wiped the coffee from the counter. "How exactly did you end up with the 'Dark Knight'?" Tempe asked using the name they'd tagged him with after he'd been introduced. "And hey, Aurora was on target, wasn't she? I mean, 'sexy, dark, dangerous, stranger'?"

Montana's head tipped to the side and her eyes drifted down lazily as she contemplated how much to tell Tempe. "She didn't mention 'sexy'. And don't forget the 'evil from your lover's past'."

Tempe rolled her eyes. "Come on… dish."

Montana plopped into the chair across from Tempe. "He asked me to dance," Montana said. "A minuet." She shook her head. "And then… he had the band play some rock songs. Apparently, he's quite the music lover. I think rock is his favorite, for training at least." Montana knew the smile was back on her face. She couldn't seem to help herself. "He called me… Victoria."

She kept the rest to herself for now, holding it close, not because she didn't trust Tempe but… she guessed she just wanted to savor it a while longer. She *did* trust Tempe, but there was the little matter of the almost throw-down earlier. She'd have to ask Aurora about it, or perhaps Conor. He'd been around a while. A while, *ha*. "He told me he'd lived through all of the centuries of music he'd requested. I figured one of them at least, went back to 300 BC."

"Wow." Tempe's eyes were orbs of dimming blue gray. Her head angled to the side. "I've been meaning to ask, what is your real name? I've never heard of anyone except states and western characters on movies called Montana, and certainly not any 'POPs'."

"This is confidential. If you tell anyone..." Montana teased, but closed her eyes, jaw muscles working, and sneered, "Branislava."

She shook her head when Tempe squealed, "You're kidding. How..."

"Don't even say it. I got sick of being called the innocuous, 'Bran', or even worse, 'Brannie', and one hapless male had the stupidity to call me 'Slave'. Well, "who's sorry now?" she sang.

"But '*Montana*'... how did that fix things?" Tempe asked.

"Having a name that was imbued with meaning, my sense of who I was and needed to be, just felt right."

"Well, what does it mean? Is it like *wild west* speak for kicking ass?"

Montana snickered, "You're not far off. Remember that movie about twenty years ago with the blonde actress? Sharon..."

"Oh, *the Quick and the Dead*. Yeah! I can see that. Sharon Stone with black hair, only instead of two fast guns on your hips, you carry needles, and a sword, but the attitude fits." Tempe smiled. If Montana were the star of her own movie it would probably be *Part II, Quicker and Deadlier* with her catch phrase, *This is gonna suck, Wife-beater*. Sharon Stone's character had nothing on Montana.

"Conor…" Montana caught Tempe's look. "…Flambé said Victoria suited me better."

"Really?" Tempe asked.

Montana looked toward the front door as someone knocked and they heard a familiar voice.

# CHAPTER 7

Jack didn't know what kind of reception he'd get when he found Tempe. He could only imagine what she'd felt, her conclusions she'd reached at the scene she'd witnessed. It had been shocking to say the least, especially when it interrupted the best sex of his life, lovemaking so extraordinary that he was unprepared to describe it in words even now.

Shocked was an inadequate word, in comparison to how he'd felt when he'd opened his front door to see Georgeanne on the porch. His vision had grayed out around the edges and for a minute he'd actually feared he was going to pass out, something he'd never done in his days as a Navy pilot even under the pressure of all those G forces. In the back of his mind maybe he'd been worried that Tempe would be left to deal with *her*. He couldn't believe he'd had even that much of a grasp on his situation when the witch had locked her wirey arms around his neck, and hadn't allowed him to push her away.

He'd placed his hands on her shoulders and pushed gently, that is to say, he deliberately, carefully—non-violently *with herculean effort*—set her away from him, outside, on the porch. He'd felt violence rise though. She wasn't going to violate his and Jordie's space ever again. He thought of Tempe once more, but before he could look for her, he had to get rid of Georgeanne. He called a cab—huh, *the* cab, to take her wherever she wanted to go, preferably the other side of the world. She'd find out soon enough there were no accommodations in Destiny. *Yes*! *Finally a perk.* He didn't care where she wound up.

As the cab pulled away from the curb, Jack began searching the house. His fears had been justified. Tempe was gone. But how? Guilt slammed into him. She must have taken off on foot and he still couldn't go after her. Not yet. He had to get to Jordie.

Fear snaked through him, the hair on his skin standing up as a new thought struck him. She could have told the driver to drive to his parents'. He'd raced to his car and driven to their house resisting the urge to flip on the sirens, though he had used his flashing lights, then, in the driveway, he'd settled in to wait.

"Daddy, what are you doing out here? Why didn't you come in?"

Jack jerked. He must have dozed after he'd parked in the driveway of his parents' house. Scrubbing his hands across his face, he pasted on a smile. "I didn't want to wake you up. Do you have plans today?" He yawned and looked at his watch—a little after seven.

She frowned into the window at him. "I have basketball practice this afternoon. I was just going to ride my bike home and fix you breakfast, but I wasn't sure, uh…"

Jack chuckled. "Get in." Tempe had been right about Jordie. She was mature and had already given some thought to who might still be at his house this morning after his date last night. She'd been as excited as Tempe. His smile dimmed though, when he thought about the news he had to deliver. Jordie wasn't going to be happy about restrictions on her activities.

"What is it?" Jordie asked, as they pulled away from his parents' house. "Oh, God, Daddy, did you blow it?"

"Blow it! What do you mean—no. No, I made you proud. With all the advice you gave me, I couldn't help but succeed. Tempe was struck speechless by the limo, the driver, and yours truly in his Navy tails."

"Oh yeah? I hope you got pictures." Her eyes lit and she clapped her hands together excitedly. "What about you? What kind of night did you have?" she waggled her eyebrows, or attempted to. Jordie was one of those girls with perfectly shaped but non-animating brows.

"Let's just say the word of the night was *thunderstruck.*

She was the most beautiful woman at the ball, hands down." He sighed, looking off. He dreaded this.

"Okay… so what's the problem? What are you doing here when you should be enjoying breakfast with your lady?" Okay, so she wasn't *that* mature. Thank God.

He took a deep breath and started, "G—"

"No!" Jordie's hands slapped the seat beside her, eyes going wide, color draining from her face. "No, no, no, no, *no!*" she cried, and burst into tears, covering her face with her hands, then sliding them up to grip her hair she looked at Jack with desperate eyes.

Jack pulled the car over at the empty strip mall and reached for her. "Come here, sweetheart."

Jordie's breath hitched. "She always ruins everything." She whimpered into his chest, "Why now? She's left us alone for two years." Raising her face, her eyes were fierce as they met his. "I wish she'd just die."

He hugged her harder. "Shh, baby, you don't mean—"

She pushed back, her expression tormented. "Oh, I do mean it. I hate her." She stared into his face, her voice choked, "Be honest, Daddy. You do, too."

Jack didn't respond because they both new his answer. But hate didn't motivate him. He was terrified of her. He'd left Memphis with Jordie and made a new life for her in Destiny. They hadn't been required to give *her* their new address after soul custody had been awarded to Jack.

He'd done everything he could to keep her from finding out where they were, but a simple search on the Internet had probably given them up, what with his campaign and election. He'd have bet his life his ex had never put her hands on a computer, which meant she'd broken pattern. She was either desperate, or driven by some motive he wasn't aware of.

He vowed she would not win at her manipulative games. She might have already cost him Tempe's trust. *Damn!* He didn't need the distraction now, with everything else that was going on. "I love you, Jordie."

Tear-filled eyes met his. "I love you, too, Daddy," distress and worry making her voice sound strangled.

He straightened. "Jordie. We are not going to allow her to affect our lives. Not ever again."

Jordie sniffed and nodded. "Tell me what happened."

Hmm, how much to explain… "Tempe was at the house and the door bell buzzed about 3 a.m. When I opened the door, she was there." *With her suitcase, and she threw her arms around my neck with Tempe standing there in my robe…* "I didn't let her in. I called a cab to take her away."

"Ha! Away. She didn't go to all this trouble to find us and then just go away. Not my m—not *that*—"

He rubbed her back and breathed out, "No. You're right. I can see we're on the same page—"

She pushed back, eyes wide, the thought just hitting her, "What did Tempe think?"

She would ask. He put his head back on the headrest as Jordie gripped his arm. "I don't know, baby. After I got rid of G, I went looking for her. She'd left."

"No! You have to go find her. Oh my God. She's going to ruin that, too!" The tears had started again, but they were tears of anger now.

Good, Jack thought. They'd devise a plan and Jordie would stick to it. She was *his* daughter after all. He'd never seen any of G's character flaws in Jordie. "Okay, here's the plan, for today at least."

Jordie had been surprisingly agreeable, until he got to the part about her not leaving the house. Then teenage desperation had supplied the perfect answer. Beffie (the Faerie dog) would guard her while Jack wasn't home, and she was sure she could enlist her friends, Andy (the teenage rebel Djinni) and Jarell (Destiny's star basketball player) to be her *body-guards*. "Wow, it sounds kind of like a Lifetime movie with me having to ask my friends to protect me from my *mother*." The word sounded like a curse, appropriately so.

Neither one of them seemed inclined to actually *speak* her name anymore. Was it some kind of magical prompting? Whatever it was, it seemed they were both tuned in. And the movie? When would he have to tell Jordie that it was much closer to a movie on the Syfy channel?

When they got back to the house, he'd fought impatience while Jordie poured them each a bowl of cereal.

He'd made sure all the windows in the house were locked. It wasn't just his law enforcement history that made him nearly immune to the feelings of guilt for locking out his daughter's own mother, but a chronicle of bad behavior by a woman who defied description or analysis. Even Beffie seemed to know what needed to be done, standing at the back door with Jordie until she locked it, then leading her back to the front door as Jack kissed her goodbye and waited for her to engage the dead bolt.

He couldn't believe they were at this point again, feeling like they were at war, on the defensive to keep from being victims of a serial maniac. Jordie was as safe as he could make her. God help him, he'd even told her where his spare gun was since he knew she would only go near it if it were a last resort. They'd both agreed, he needed to find Tempe and explain.

So he'd driven to the old Plantation. It was dark, and though Tempe's truck sat in the driveway, she wasn't home. Where would she go? Which of her friends was within walking distance, he wondered. He didn't care about the dress but he did grimace at the thought of her walking the streets barefoot.

He'd called her cellphone, but it had gone straight to voicemail, and he couldn't come close to explaining the situation in ten seconds or less, so he just hung up. He ran down the list of her friends—the SOAPs. Tops on her list would have been either Aurora or Montana. In the back of his mind, he considered that she might have run to—looked for— Dylan, but he rejected that. He decided on Montana.

～

JACK KNOCKED ON THE WIDE ARCHED DOOR OF Montana's home. "Montana, Tempe?"

The curtain slid back from the front window and he caught a glimpse of Tempe's sparkling dress just as the door was flung outward by a very unfriendly looking Montana… What was her last name anyway?

"Montana, I need to see Tempe."

Montana's eyes narrowed and she crossed her arms. *Hmm*, this wasn't good. Maybe Tempe had told her she didn't want to speak to him. He called, "Tempe, can we talk?" but kept his eyes on Montana whose body language was shouting, *Come one inch closer and see what you get, Lawman.*

Jack stood his ground but recognized Tempe's thunder from inside the room. Montana turned, swung the door wide and Tempe appeared at the door. "Jack, come in."

He had to step around Montana since she was still halfway blocking the doorway. "What's wrong with her?" he asked Tempe, pointing his thumb at her over his shoulder as Tempe led the way to the kitchen.

"Nothing is wrong with me, Sheriff," Montana said. "I care about my friends…"

"I do too, Montana. Look, can I talk to Tempe, alone? This is really none of your business."

That didn't go over well. The next second Jack was on his ass; Montana was standing over him, hair flying, blue eyes glaring, a sword aimed at his throat. "What the hell?" Where had that thing come from?

# CHAPTER 8

Jack stared up at Montana from the terra-cotta floor. What was it with all the swords lately? *Menori* grumbled, or in her case thundered, and Jack looked from Tempe to Montana. He frowned.

Montana's eyes squinted at Tempe, then looked at Jack.

Tempe jumped in, "Actually it is her business, Jack. Montana, is what's known as a Dinnshencha. She was simply following her nature."

"Montana," Tempe spoke to the woman who looked more like Conan than an emergency responder. "He would never hurt me." Her hand pushed the sword down toward the floor and Montana relaxed *slightly*.

"Is that like a female Seal?" Jack asked, rubbed his tail-bone and got to his feet, still eyeing the massive sword. He looked for a sheath or strap but saw none. "I don't have to ask if she's dangerous, do I?"

"She's dangerous, but only to men."

Jack's eyebrows lifted, "Oh, now, I feel better."

"Bad men and bad POPS. When a woman is threatened, Montana can shift into anything to defend her."

"Anything covers a lot. Ever seen her in action?" he asked.

Tempe frowned. "I've seen her do some incredible things in her human form."

"Hel*lo*, standing here, listening," the amazon said nearby.

Jack said, "Oh, I thought you were still on standby in automatic strike mode. Your eyes are still a little iced over." Jack was trying to lighten Montana's mood but he guessed she just had to be sure of his intentions before her protective switch flipped to off.

Montana shrugged and Jack said, "I need to talk to Tempe, to explain—"

Montana said, "So talk."

Jack sighed, plowed his hand through his hair—it didn't appear to be the first time—and turned to Tempe.

Tempe rose, rubbing her arms as if she were nervous or chilled. "You don't owe me an explanation, Jack. Really. If I were in your place I'd do the same thing. I'd try to make it work, put my family back together, if for no other reason than for my daughter—"

He grabbed her arms and held her hard. "God, is that what you think?"

Montana's huge sword flashed between them. Jack glared at her. "Dammit, Montana, don't you have something to do, like..." he looked around... "clean up—jeez, what happened here?"

Reluctantly, Montana withdrew, looking at Tempe, "I'll be in the kitchen, but if you need me..." then at Jack.

Jack called, "She won't need you," to Montana's retreating form.

"I don't know what to think, Jack," Tempe said, but she smiled at his growing familiarity with her non-human friends. He probably didn't even realize it. "Let's walk outside." She led the way onto the wide porch to a swing covered with an old woven blanket. She pulled it around her. Jack frowned. She'd told him she didn't feel atmospheric changes, like heat and cold.

"Tempe, my crazy ex doesn't deserve any of the time devoted to talking about her." He blew out a breath, hooking one thumb in his gun belt. "But that's SOP with crazy people isn't it?"

Her brows hiked and she gave a little snort, "Watch it. Not so long ago you had me in that category, remember?"

"Well, I've got experience and perspective since then," he smiled, again hoping she could see how he was feeling without having to explain. He wasn't hiding his feelings; he just wasn't sure how to put them into words. "I had a talk with myself Friday before we rescued River. I decided there's *cool crazy*, that's you and a few others I've met lately, and then there's *deranged*, calculating and…that's… my ex."

"You still don't call her by name," Tempe said frowning and he had to give her the truth.

"Have you ever known people you suspected were just plain evil?" Her eyes squinted thoughtfully. All his adult life he'd felt silly for even thinking it. "For years now, it seemed like when I use her name, I'm calling her to me and Jordie—calling up evil—giving her power. I know that sounds…"

"It's not odd at all, Jack; darkness is real, and names do have power especially in some communities, magical ones. I was just thinking about something Aurora told me last night at the ball. She said I would 'meet evil from my lover's past soon'. I thought she meant Dylan because, well, we hadn't…"

"Made love?" he offered. "But she didn't call her by name, I take it."

"Aurora said it wasn't clear, that the approach of Paramoon had confused her scrying." She saw the clueless look he gave her. "Readings," she added. "She does something with that pearlescent bowl and her crystals. It's the first time I've ever seen it."

"So is that because she's losing power?"

"I don't know. Remember, I've just come fully into the Paramortal loop myself, and I'm as clueless as you in some respects." He started to comment but she said, "I'm not beating myself up. Just accepting the truth. You should talk to Aurora. I can't tell you much, and even if I knew, it's not up to me to reveal the identity of Paramortals you don't already know. She'll know who might be of some help."

"I'm sorry about this morning." He looked up toward the clouds and the light drifting snow then his eyes lowered to hers. "The very last thing I'd consider in this lifetime would be reconciling or even living in the same state as that maniacal self-centered manipulator. The only reason I didn't take her to New Orleans and put her on a flight to Antarctica was that it would be a waste of time. For years, I lived in fear that she would show up from one of her 'trips' and steal Jordie away or turn her against me somehow."

He shoved off the stool and paced. "Tempe, I can understand if you don't want to have anything to do with me until she's out of the picture. Shit, I could understand if you didn't want to risk having any future contact with her, but I'm hoping you're made of sterner stuff than that. I could say it's because Jordie likes you and you're good for her. But I'm the one that's tired of giving in, tired of looking over our shoulders and putting off relationships because of her. I want a chance to see where this relationship can lead."

Tempe looked unsure. He still hadn't given her many

details about his marriage. Tempe might think he didn't trust her. "Would you at least say something?" he asked quietly. "I've kind of put myself out there…"

"If she's so bad, how did you end up married to her?" she asked.

# CHAPTER 9

Jack winced. "I wish I could make it sound romantic, or even touching—boy goes off to war leaving his mourning girlfriend behind waiting. Honestly, it was more about a boy getting ready to deploy overseas on his first tour, with too much testosterone, and a fear of dying.

"When I entered basic, I was away from home, getting ready to deploy. You vacillate between thinking you'll live forever and knowing you might not come home.

"She was at a party some of the officers threw and came at me really hard. One time! I slept with her and didn't even remember it. One time, and except for the joy of having Jordie in my life, the rest has been teetotal hell. When Jordie was three I came home on leave and she begged me to let her go live with my parents. She..." Jack cleared his throat. "She said her mother didn't love her."

74

Jack's eyes burned into hers. "She shouldn't have even been old enough to figure that out. My next stint overseas was interminable. My parents had to keep their eyes on G because I wasn't able to hire a private investigator until I came home again. If it hadn't been for them, I'd have gone AWOL to get home to Jordie. But G wasn't interested in being a mother. She stayed gone more than she was home, and my parents were always around whenever she was with Jordie. None of us trusted her."

Jack's eyes narrowed, "When other soldiers were having nightmares about the enemy, I was planning how to extricate myself from *her* and having nightmares about coming home and finding Jordie gone.

"Keep your enemy close, was our mantra. We kept our eyes on her until I got the packet from my private investigator. It held some very bizarre, very incriminating evidence. Three years ago, we went before a judge. I got full custody, and an annulment. We've only seen her once since then, in Memphis, when she showed up wanting money and saying she wanted to take Jordie…" he visibly shivered… "on a trip."

"Where, and with what?"

"Yeah. I'd left the service and was working in Memphis for the police department so I had resources to keep Jordie covered. She finally gave up and left. I had hopes that she got remarried or run over by a train." He shrugged, "I don't know what to do except protect Jordie. At least she's old enough now to be part of the plan. Beffie's standing guard right now."

"Where is G?"

"I called THE TAXI. I was shook up."

"Does she have somewhere to go?"

"You know, Scarlet, frankly—" He breathed a tired sigh, one corner of his mouth canted. "But, here we are. Jordie says we found our *destiny*." He took Tempe's hand, turning serious, "It's like we were meant to be here. Can you believe I just said that?"

She said, "I was afraid, Jack. I... care about you. You know my history, with my father and Dylan. Trusting a man isn't something I do easily. I have wonderful friends..."

"Some a little more protective than others..." he murmured good-naturedly.

Tempe smiled. "I guess I'm lucky that way, too, huh?" Her head tilted and her eyelids floated down briefly. When they opened they regarded him softly. Damn, she was pretty. Even in her bedraggled gown. It was probably ruined and he had only himself to blame. She'd literally walked out into the night. He'd found her shoes in the living room which just made it worse, not that she could have walked anywhere in them. Maybe he could have the shoes bronzed or something, if she forgave him.

"I'm sorry, Sweetheart." Jack said. "Don't let *her* ruin what was an extraordinary night."

Tempe wondered aloud, "The date or the sex?"

"All of it. Tell me you'll give us another chance." Jack moved in to her, his hand cupping her cheek, "I need you."

His beautiful silver green eyes stared down into hers. There was no smile, no prevarication, just sincerity. She smiled at him. It was the first time a man had said those three words to her, *I need you.* "I think I love you, Jack."

His eyes crinkled then, the lines she imagined had formed during all those sorties, squinting at the bright sky, but now she knew they'd probably been put there from worry. He was a fine man, and she didn't know how she'd doubted him.

She *hadn't* doubted *him* really. She'd doubted *herself.*

"I *know* I love you, Tempe." His face softened and he hugged her, then the intensity in his gaze was reflected in the prominent nudge she felt against her stomach. His mouth descended on hers and they briefly allowed themselves a kiss that seemed to answer any leftover questions, and promise more for later.

"I NEED TO TALK TO MONTANA." JACK RESTED HIS CHIN on Tempe's head while his lower body adjusted to the new plan of action. "What did you call her? A Dinche? Was it my imagination last night or did she look like she was about to eat me alive in front of everybody?"

"She did look a little on edge there for a bit, but there's a reason for that. She perceived a threat to the families she's charged with defending."

"Charged by whom?" he asked. He was the sheriff of the parish and knew most of the authorities around the lake and statewide.

"Zeus."

"Ha! That's a good one." Tempe's unique curses came to mind, but she wasn't smiling. "You're serious. Zeus? As in Greek mythology?"

"He's not a myth."

"So is that where your power comes from?"

She only hesitated briefly. It was a mark of how much things had changed between them that she just shrugged and smiled. "Pretty much."

He blew out a breath scrubbing his scalp with his fingers, as if that would help him understand this world. "All right let's table that for later, and go find Montana."

MONTANA HAD BEEN BUSY WHILE THEY'D BEEN OUTSIDE. Fresh coffee sat on the counter and everything had been put to rights. Jack looked over at Montana who lifted her sword from its perch by the wall, and for some reason the color of her eyes when she turned struck him…

"The *Denche. Tanker,*" the Bentson woman had said. *Thank the Dinnshencha.*

He shook his head. "You weren't by any chance at a domestic abuse scene on Saturday at 0300 where someone took out a wife beater in a rather unique fashion." His eyes narrowed on hers, and on the sword. She rolled her eyes, tossed the sword on her couch and said, "I didn't touch the guy."

Jack smiled, "Ah, so you were there. If you didn't kill him then you must have been the one sliding around in the blood." She didn't blink. "No comment?"

Montana's gaze narrowed. Tempe looked from Jack to Montana. Jack said, "Good thing the victim had stowed her cat in the other room." Finally, a tiny reaction from Montana.

Jack sobered. "Did you turn into a mouse because you lacked the power to turn into anything larger, because of the Para-moon?"

"Not exactly."

Tempe said, "Someone want to fill me in?"

Montana said, "I was on a domestic abuse call and Jack responded. I had to change twice, the second time into something small and fast. Luckily Mr. Wildlife Lover here helped me escape. He might not have if he'd seen me in my gator skin."

Jack asked, "So what happened to the abuser?"

"If I told you—"

"You'd have to kill me?" Jack hmmphed, "Heard it…"

"…not me, but someone else might." It was obvious she didn't intend to explain further.

Jack stroked a hand over Tempe's head. "What's happened to your hair? The coincidence?"

Tempe's head tilted as she pulled a strand around to look at it, glancing over at Montana. "My hair?"

"Yes, the streaks are gone and your hair isn't bright like it was. Do you feel okay?" His hand went to her cheek, and Montana restrained herself with effort.

"I think I can still rumble a bit," Tempe said, her eyes narrowing on Jack. "Why?"

He turned to Montana, "Is your power gone?"

Montana shrugged and didn't look at him directly, as if she didn't want to give away her true status. "I still have some moves."

Tempe asked, "But you can't shift?" She didn't seem to want to answer Jack's question directly.

Montana breathed out harsh sigh, "No, I can't shift but I can still fight, and as you can see I still have Mathilda, my sword shifter. For now, and, then… there's my other side."

"Other side?" Jack asked.

"Oh, right," said Tempe, slapping her forehead. Montana nodded. Tempe turned to Jack, "Mont—"

"I'm part vampire."

# CHAPTER 10

Jack almost took a step back but as Dylan had said, Jack hadn't thrived under pressure on a fluke, though his mind was probably replaying every vampire movie from *Lestat* to *Van Helsing*. He raised his eyebrows and blinked. "You mean like sucking blood, pointy fangs... how does that work exactly in real life?" He looked Montana over, searching for fangs and claws?

Montana gave a deep throaty chuckle. "Oh, Jack, you're just too much fun. It's not all bad. You're seeing me during the day right? No fangs, no scalding or turning to ash." She sighed, "My hereditary nature is Dinnshencha; I am a warrior, and I can still fight like one, with Mathilda or my body. I can no longer shift until the end of the Para-moon, but I'll still be stronger than most men because nothing celestial or magical can affect my vampire."

"How can someone be part vampire?"

"The majority of vampires surviving today were made that way by a bite, either voluntarily or involuntarily. Most, like me are a kind of hybrid. The change may have come about to save one's life, or it could have been consensual as it was in my case many years ago. I chose that vampire for his strength of blood and mind. He complemented my Dinnshencha. Not all part vampires are created equal, *ye ken?*" She laughed at her private joke. Jack and Tempe looked at each other.

"Does this mean you'll have to like... suck blood now?" Tempe asked. Jack's eyebrows rose so high into his hairline, Tempe wondered if they'd get stuck there.

Again, Montana chuckled and kept her eyes on Jack, "Yes, I'll have to feed." Jack choked. She said, "It's okay, Jack. I don't need any of *your* blood." She showed him some fang, her voice lowering to a husky rasp, "I have that taken care of."

Jack said, "Look, you're obviously starting to experience some repercussions from the Para-moon and it's not even full yet. Does anyone know when the bad guys will come charging through the portal?"

Tempe and Montana stared at Jack. "I didn't know you knew about the portal, Jack," said Montana.

"You mean there's... it was just a figure of speech, something I got from *Stargate*..."

She grinned, "Just messing with you, Jack. You'll have to ask Aurora about the whens and hows and whos? My job is just taking care of them as they… come through the portal." She failed to stifle another laugh.

Jack's eyebrow lifted as if wondering about Montana's mental stability. Tempe was worried as well. Montana's sense of humor ran to sarcasm, not guffaws. "I guess I should take Tempe home and get over to Aurora's."

Montana used her sword to salute them and then, when they moved out of her way, took a stance against some invisible opponent and began dancing and thrusting.

TEMPE LOOKED OUT OF JACK'S CRUISER AS HE DROVE TO Harmony. Should she tell him who had been at Montana's? Dylan said Conor was most likely a good POP but how did they know?

Jack said, "This thing has already started. I need more Intel. Who are the bad guys? Which good guys will still be able to… function?"

Tempe struggled for a way to explain. "Do you know what Samhain is?"

"Sal, when?"

"You've probably heard it pronounced sam hane. But either way, it's a time in the fall, October 31st to be exact, when the veil between worlds is thin and um, spirits and mortals—actually, all beings—can pass easily between them."

"Hmm, kinda like that non-existent portal we were talking about. But, this is February."

"You're getting ahead of me. It's the concept I'm going for here. The Para-moon is like that, in the sense that because so many Paramortals lose their power during the coincidence between Luna and Cache, a power shift results. Many of our enemies feel free and somewhat empowered by their access to the world we protect, the people we protect."

"As well as the protectors," he said, nodding.

"True."

"So what do we do? Turn over the town to the outlaw POPs like they did in the old West?"

"I hate to keep correcting you on the POP thing because the nickname for our enemies is growing on me. It does a nice job of lumping them together." She caught him staring at her. "What is it?" She looked down, "I'm sorry for ruining the dress." Tears welled in her eyes suddenly.

"Hey," Jack said softly, reaching across the front seat to stroke her cheek. "The dress had its day. You couldn't wear it twice anyway, right? I'm the one who's sorry for not handling the situation better when G-*crazy* showed up. Don't give it another thought okay?"

She nodded as they pulled into the driveway at Harmony. Jack got out and as she turned to slip off the seat, he sidled in between her legs. He ran his hands up her arms to her shoulders, then trailed his fingers up her throat to her face, holding it between his large hands. "That's not what I was looking at, Tempe. I asked you at Montana's how you're feeling."

She looked up into his concerned eyes, his bronze streaked hair brushing his collar, his *official* demeanor a thing of the past. "I'm fine. I just feel kind of tired. Neither one of us got any sleep last night."

He frowned, "Can you tell if your powers are gone? Have you tried to call *menori* lately? I heard some thunder at Montana's."

She took his hand and led him toward the door. When they made it to the porch, she turned and concentrating, attempted to lock the doors on his cruiser. She squeezed her eyes shut, and finally she heard the thunk of the locks engaging. She swayed.

Jack scooped her up and walked inside. "I guess that answers my question." He walked into the foyer and Tempe pushed the door shut behind them—with her hand.

"Put me down in the kitchen, please. I'll make us a cup of coffee." When he stopped, she slid down his body to the counter top, resting her head against his chest. "You're about to get your wish," she said, her voice muffled into his flannel shirt.

"What wish is that?" he asked.

"A completely human, completely ordinary girlfriend, as normal as I'll ever be. Hopefully, I'll still be here after the big switch goes back on." His breathing stumbled briefly beneath her cheek.

"I have no wish for anyone ordinary, Sweetheart... or completely human. You've kinda grown on me. Why wouldn't you be here?" He hoped his voice sounded steadier, braver, than he felt. There was a real chance he could lose her before they ever had a chance at more.

"Well," her voice was soft, "Bad guys with power, good guys without... can't be good."

Jack had been thinking about the impending crisis, what did they call it? *Chaos*, what a name. How would he be able to fight off bad POPs with only a handful of human deputies? "I'm not going to let anything happen to you, Tempest Pomeroy."

He bent his head and set his lips to hers, his tongue entering slowly to caress hers while his hands stroked her back. It was affectionate, sweetly sensual and it promised his complete devotion and protection. She got the message, smiling into his kiss.

"What is it?" he asked, his head tilting back as he looked down at her. "Did I do it wrong?"

"I think you know your kisses dazzle me. I just can't help but look back at how far we've come in such a short time." She sobered. "I do love you, Jack, and I don't want you to think if things don't turn out—"

"Stop. I love you, too, Tempe, but I've been watching you and Montana, and I think the Para-moon is affecting more than abilities. I'm new at this supernatural thing but I'm good at detecting changes, observing. If I'm right, your emotions are being amplified, and your reasoning could be affected as well. So just do whatever you can to stay positive for me, okay?"

He kissed her again; this time it was a quick, hot suggestion of more than just devotion and protection. "Until later, Darlin'. I'm headed to Aurora's. Why don't you get a nap, and I'll come back later and let you know about the big plan?"

Tempe's smile disappeared as she watched his taillights go down the street. She didn't seem to have any positive vibes left. Maybe he was right. Maybe the moons were to blame. She sat down on the couch and put her head back. In just a few minutes she'd get up and make that cup of coffee.

# CHAPTER 11

Dylan approached the swamp listening for further cries or evidence of whatever had made the sound. He was absolutely sure it wasn't Katerina. For the first time in many years feelings for a woman were stirring inside of him. Oh, he hadn't lied to Tempe; he'd loved her in a way, but he realized now that there'd been a lot of feelings balled up in that situation—his affection for her having seen her grow up, his friendship with her parents, the protectiveness guardians feel for their charges.

He rolled his eyes. He was sounding like some kind of pervert, but in their world once someone went through his or her quickening, they were pretty much on their way to being old souls. Ancient beings mated with younger ones every day with no thought to how long they'd been around.

His feelings for Katerina were different. He wasn't her guardian and yet he felt protective. They'd made love for the first time since he'd known her and it made him feel stronger, more willing to put his feelings out there. It was still too soon though as she had secrets she wasn't willing, or didn't feel safe enough to share. Then she'd tried to bite his head off like one of those insects that devours its partner after mating. Mating. That word held a bit more import than Dylan wanted to think about right now. Besides, it didn't turn out too well for the insect's better half.

If they all made it through the Para-moon he would have to persuade Katerina to tell him about her past and how she'd wound up in Destiny six months earlier.

Dylan's eyesight, usually so preternaturally keen, was now only equal to a human's fresh from the Lasix surgeon. Not only was his eyesight suffering, but he missed being able to divine almost everything with just his nose. Normally he could determine time of day, distinguish locations and track any creatures as easily as most people simply put one foot in front of the other.

He didn't like this feeling at all. It didn't matter to him that it had a limited time span. What could happen in a mere twenty-four hours made his bones chill just to contemplate. Unfortunately, that was part of his job as a guardian. Determine the worst case and strategize to limit the disastrous consequences, and protect the community and his charge from danger until power returned.

But his strategizing gene seemed to have lost its way, along with his charge-into-the-enemy's-camp fearlessness. Contemplating going into the water to investigate that whirlpool action fifty yards in front of him would have been a Disney experience for him prior to this morning.

He'd personally experienced the last Para-moon, but as a child. He hadn't gone through his Vyal K'allanti yet so the Para-moon didn't affect him like it did others. He remembered though. His father had been killed during the power down by a variant who'd hidden in the guise of a human friend until the height of the eclipse...

Water sloshed against the bank and a low groan like squeaky hinges on a ship's hull came closer. He waded into the water and dived while he could still feel a smidgeon of his power. Trained in under water rescue and possessing supernatural lungs, Dylan thought he could manage this even without being able to shift into Finrir. He hoped.

The soft gray light of morning filtered through the water with some areas being more cloudy than clear, probably due to the activity in front of him. He saw something large, though it might have been an under-water berm or fallen cypress tree. Scavenging under-water was second nature to Dylan and he rooted around in the muck near some cypress knees and tested the water depth by lowering his legs to the murky bottom.

There was about a foot and a half of sludge at the bottom and the depth must be around six or seven feet because it covered his head when he dug his feet down into the muck. He flapped his hands to rise through the water surface enough to get another breath but not to call attention to himself, if the creature couldn't see him. He was sure now—it wasn't Kat. Lions and water...

He saw the bulky shape up ahead and considered trying to change to Finrir, since that form took less oxygen, but now was not the time to wind up as a vulnerable half-shifted man-bear. He kicked and surfaced briefly, taking another deep breat,h but before he could dive he saw the deep fast-moving rush of waves and felt something bump against his hip, then clamp around his knees.

HE CLENCHED HIS MOUTH SHUT AS HE WAS PULLED beneath the water's surface. When whatever had a hold of him stopped, he should be able to get purchase on the bottom and force whoever it was to let him go.

But the *whoever* was a *whatever,* and its intention seemed to be to drag him down into the silty debris-laden bottom. He struggled to pull his legs free knowing his efforts would deplete his oxygen more quickly. The thing was strong.

Feeling for its limbs, grasping for a handhold... appendages, the head, eyes, tender joints, he felt only a rough hide and spiny ridge like wings with razor sharp tips he needed to avoid. At one point he thought he had his hand on its head but the dome felt... weird... like a rock or faceted stone. It plowed into the bottom, dragging him through it and practically sitting on him, pressing him face first into the mud.

This was bad. If he were above the water he might have taken a deep breath to calm himself. He resisted the urge to do that knowing he must breathe out if minutely to keep the water from forcing its way into his nose and then his lungs.

He was starting to feel the effects of his struggles, his air getting low, legs still trapped by the beast. He had no idea what form it would take out of the water, as it was impossible for him to determine *what* it was, the way it held itself and held him. It was powerful, and it was much too large to remain hidden beneath the shallow waters of the Forge for long.

So, did the Para-moon have something to do with it being here, or was its appearance merely coincidental. Was it in league with their enemy or some kind of lone wolf? *Now's a helluva time to start thinking analytically, Dylan.* And those questions would be moot before long as he was about to either gasp out of desperation and swallow a lungful of bayou slime, or his lungs would collapse.

Desperation hit first. He pushed against the creature's sides with his hands and twisted to free his legs but it wasn't happening. He squirmed frantically but to no avail. The thing must weigh a couple tons and only the water's buoyancy kept it from crushing him. Maybe he should play dead. Well, before long he would be.

Fuzzily his hand came up to cover his nose and mouth, trying to avoid taking in water, but as the fog eased across his senses he knew that of course, he wouldn't be able to hold his nose in unconsciousness and then, he would drown.

At least he knew it wasn't Katerina. Beautiful, dark, sleek Kat. Too bad he wouldn't get a chance to see her again, to save her... from her past. And he hated... hated...

His hand slipped off the spiny ridge of leathery skin as his mind drifted and the other floated away from his face. The reflex of his parched lungs was to fill, taking in their first wash of dirty swamp water. Then, everything went black.

# CHAPTER 12

Seconds or minutes later he came awake violently, coughing, spewing foul swamp detritus. Opening his eyes as water drained from his limbs, he realized he was being lifted out of the swamp, and was looking down at the ridged back of the creature from twenty feet in the air. Hadn't he, just seconds before, been in the clutches of a large creature of indeterminable species?

He blinked eyes filmed over with grit and slime and started squirming, then thought better of it because, really, he didn't want to end up back in the water with that thing. His arms felt like they were about to be jerked out of their sockets. His feet flew around under him as the crane or whatever had saved him swung him toward land. As soon as the bank came into view the operator simply opened its jaws and dropped him to the ground below.

Dylan groaned as he crossed his arms over his chest,

squeezing his triceps to massage the pain. Something nudged his ribs and, afraid the swamp *thang* had followed him out of the water, he rolled away from the edge. He coughed and spewed the foul tasting water until he thought he'd spew up his very lungs.

The nudge came again and when he opened his slimy eyes, his vision was dark. Had he been blinded? If he were Finrir he could heal, but without that nature available to him, it would go with him eternally. He panicked. Then the darkness moved, gray sky entered his field of vision and he got a glimpse of his savior.

Not a crane. But it definitely had jaws. Dylan's eyes widened as he looked into the face? Snout? Teeth— certainly—of the biggest baddest looking black dragon he'd ever seen. It looked down at him benignly, which made sense because a dragon his size certainly wouldn't be worried about a little bedraggled, powerless Finrir.

Although, maybe he was inferring the wrong thing from that look. Maybe he was about to be lunch. Dylan thought from the tilt of the dragon's head and the one eye open wider than the other, he'd been considered for an appetizer and found wanting.

The dragon's long toothy snout lowered until it was so close, Dylan could make out the fine edge of red around its lips and nostrils. Its eyes, the color of live flames, swirled. *Uh-oh.* He rose up on his elbows preparing to crab walk away when the roar came again.

Dylan looked toward the sound and the dragon looked

as well, but his expression didn't change. Not much affected him it seemed. And why should it? Surely, his kind, if there were more—and that was a terrifying thought—were the largest on Earth.

"So it wasn't you," Dylan said, when it dawned on him that this giant black mass of Dragondom hadn't been the creature in the swamp. Either his mind was fogged from the power down and being held under until he'd nearly kicked it, or it was addled from the abrupt fall from those fearsome jaws. Of course it hadn't been him. No way he could hide that gargantuan body in a six-foot deep swamp.

He backed up when fire more or less drizzled from the dragon's nostrils as it looked off toward the sound and back at Dylan. Dylan could have sworn the expression on the dragon's face was something akin to, *Duh, you think you dragged yourself out?*

Reluctantly Dylan said, "Thanks. That is unless you saved me to eat me," *that* with a questioning lilt to his words.

The air shimmered and Dylan felt, more than saw the dragon shift, it happened so fast. In front of him stood a warrior. This had to be the Knight Tempe mentioned since the swords were unlike anything Dylan had ever seen.

His eyes and the surrounding skin were almost as black as his scales, and his long hair. Across his powerful shoulders were raised tattoos. His wrists, waist and feet were encased in tool worked bronze and pewter, and the hilts of those shiny crenelated sword edges were flashing visibly behind his head. He wondered briefly where all that metal went when he changed.

Dylan remembered his conversation with Tempe. She'd asked if he knew a Samurai Knight. This Knight was no Samurai. And anyone seeing the leathery tatts on his shoulders probably mistook them for bat wings, to their eternal surprise.

The Knight stared down at Dylan, then held out his hand. It was huge and square, the bronze skin smooth, not leathery or scaled as Dylan would have expected. He was not the first dragon Dylan had met, but he was by far the biggest.

"Come, mon, do you wish to lie there like a *big Jessie* until that Vouivre comes back? If so, I'll be g'win. I ha'e important business at the golf course."

The long fingers moved once to remind Dylan he was dealing with an impatient dragon, with *appointments to keep (and a thousand miles before he could sleep)*. *Oh boy, he was losing it*. He took the Knight's hand. From the strength of his grip he figured this dragonman could have easily sent him flying through the air and back into the swamp. Standing, he was nearly eye-to-eye with the warrior. "What's this business you spoke of? Who are you?"

A smile kicked up on one side of the enigmatic face. "Yer welcome, lad. I'm on my way to help a pal. Conor de Sept Flambé at your service." He canted his head in a slight nod.

"Dylan McGuinness. Not to be nosy, but it's part of being an investigator—who's your pal? Didn't you just get here?" He doubted there was anywhere in Destiny this big humping dragon could have hidden for long. And he didn't know of any other dragons in Destiny.

"Come wit' me and I'll tell you aboot him."

"How do you plan to get to the golf course, walk?"

Flambé just stared at Dylan, his eyes shooting him an *if-you-can't-figure-that-one-out* look. Dylan could just see it. Sunday morning, people leaving church, getting ready to go to the park, washing their cars, and suddenly the sun goes dark. They look up to see a fantasy creature from an old Matthew McConaughey movie—swooping down. They'd think *end of the world...* "Let's save the general population from mass hysteria and take my vehicle," Dylan offered.

Conor shrugged, "Suit yerself. But hurry, mon, Garric is in dire need of assistance."

Dylan led the Knight to his SUV not bothering to ask what he'd do with the swords. Some topics should probably be avoided. "Who's this Garric, anyway? And how do you know him—you've been here how long?"

"Since Saturday morn." Dylan floored the SUV taking off in the direction of Enchanted Glen. "Garric is a Paramortal shifter, like yourself. Not Finrir. With the

Para-moon, he needs to be in his den to survive his recent unfortunate circumstances. As it is, not being able to shift, the healing will be prolonged."

Dylan frowned. "I don't know any shifters that live around the golf course."

"Not around, *on*. You know him as Lancelot."

# CHAPTER 13

DYLAN KNEW HIS MOUTH WAS HANGING OPEN. SHAKING himself, because it was embarrassing appearing so uninformed to this dragon. "A shifter gator? I thought Lancelot was down at LSU. The super-vets down there were hoping to save him."

Conor cursed and smoke accumulated in the cab. "They were about to kill him. He escaped and manage to nearly make it back to his den, but the moons have affected his strength and shifting abilities."

"What did you call that thing in the swamp? Did you see it? All I saw was a huge mass under water. It felt like it had spiny fins, and it was trying to smother me in the muck." Even to his own ears, Dylan thought he sounded like a toddler. *How? Why? Who? Why now? Whah, whah.* He was so not himself.

"The creature was Le Vouivre. She is a cousin, a dragonFae of the four elements. Don't confuse her with the others," Flambé said.

What did that mean? What others? Dylan wondered. "Why is this gator so important?"

"Why is *any* being important?" was Conor's response, which more than anything he'd heard so far convinced him this was one of Jack's good POPs. *Yay*. Jack was going to need help.

Dylan looked out his window. The dragon Knight was playing it close to his scaly vest. "Look, you can trust me…"

Flambé's eyes tracked to Dylan's as if they controlled the direction of his face as well; cool, black eyes that gave nothing away, kind of like Dylan's demeanor had been everyday since his quickening *with the exception of today.* "If I weren't sure of that, Finrir, I would have let Le Vouivre smother you. You ken?"

Dylan did ken, and making fists around the steering wheel resisted either a shiver or a retort.

They passed the last mile in a tacit uncommunicative quiet.

THE PARKING LOT AT THE CLUBHOUSE WAS EMPTY SO Dylan parked in front. By the time he got out of the car, Conor was already walking toward the fairway.

"Flambé, do you know where you're going?"

The Knight placed one foot down, then placed the other next to it deliberately and turned. Dylan got the feeling he was doing a mental eye roll.

"Well, *how* do you know where you're going?" This time *dragonman* ignored the questions, resuming his steady pace along the cart path at the side of the clubhouse. Dylan jogged up next to him, matching him stride for long stride.

The guy gave new meaning to the word stoic, and Dylan mourned the loss of the "dark and scary" tag which he'd maintained sole possession of until today. *Guess it goes to show there's always someone badder out there than you.* Disconcerting thought what with the power down and beings like this Vouivre in town. And what had the Knight meant by "Don't confuse her with the others?"

*Her?* With his mind racing, Dylan didn't realize Flambé had stopped walking until he nearly sliced his nose off on one of the menacing swords. He stepped around him and saw what had caused the warrior to stop mid-stride.

A very large redheaded naked man lay on the fairway. He was face down, his strapping arms lying next to tree trunk sized thighs as if he hadn't even attempted to break his fall.

"Is this… Garric?" asked Dylan.

Conor nodded. "Yes. Git'his legs."

"How do you know him?" Dylan knew he was sounding like Chatty Cathy but he was feeling a little like Jack now. Getting hit with this much new information as long as he'd been around was a new experience.

"We need to move him to his den."

"Oh, the slew. That's what he's doing here?" Dylan wished to God he could make himself shut up but his lips seemed to move without his brain even forming the words.

The Knight's eyes did a swan dive and motioned for Dylan to get busy.

"Well, I didn't know. How come he's never shown his man form before?"

Flambé let out a breath. "He does'nae take human form unless he's ill, or during the Para-moon. In this case whatever poison the Nucklavee used, Sir Garric is still suffering from it and, unable to get to his den, he cannae heal. Now stop asking so many questions, mon, and make yerself useful." The burr was getting very pronounced and Dylan thought it might be a signal of the dragon's impending shift. He shut up.

Conor stomped around to the prone man's head, the toes of his metal plated boots even with his shoulders. Pointing at Lancelot's—Garric's—feet, he bent to turn him over. Dylan stooped to help. He appeared to be in bad shape, the coloration of his chest, face and thighs almost purple. "What now?" Dylan asked. "He doesn't look good." Dylan didn't have any idea what a sick were-gator would look like in human form, but the purple mottling on his sunken skin couldn't be normal.

"You pick up his legs. I'll get his shoulders," Conor commanded.

"Where are we taking him? Shouldn't we call a healer, an EMT, the vet?" Dylan asked.

"McGuinness, are you always so full of questions? Grab his legs and let's go."

Dylan shut-up, again. He resolved to be more like his usual self, which he figured was about as likely as an addict resolving not to snort crack, at least until after the Coincidence. He would admit he was having some issues, but he didn't intend to admit it to Flambé. That would be like a mouse sitting in front of a cobra saying, "You know I'm helpless, so eat me". He bent and picked up the heavy lower limbs of the sick were while the Knight lifted his upper torso effortlessly. He could probably carry Garric fireman style all by himself.

"Walk," *dragonman* said.

Dylan walked. He wanted to ask where they were taking him but the big man was so heavy it took all his effort to walk and not drop him. To Dylan it felt like they'd been plodding along forever. The ailing *gatorman* never stirred or moaned. Finally, the swordsman stopped and lowered the man's head to the ground. Dylan followed suit, lowering his feet, breathing hard. Dylan would have bit his tongue not to ask another question, but curiosity was killing him.

"Now to place him in his den." He pointed at the slew.

Dylan gawked, "What are you trying to do, kill him? He's hardly breathing and he's not in gator form. Won't he drown?"

Conor sighed and muttered what sounded like, "Were-bears…" under his breath, then he straddled Garric's waist, grasped his wrists pulling him forward and launched the nearly three hundred pound victim up and over his shoulder as if he weighed nothing. *Son of a bitch.* The dragon had been playing him. Dylan seethed.

"Ach, dinnae fash yerself, Finrir, we drakos must get our fun where we can, ye ken?"

He turned and with a mighty heave, tossed Garric into the slew. Dylan just stared. Conor turned toward him, "Now he will heal. The waters of his den have power."

"Oh," Dylan got it. "They tap into the Super pulse that runs through the Forge."

Conor merely nodded not making a big deal of Dylan not knowing about Garric. Thankfully.

"So what now? Why are you here, anyway? To rescue gators and Finrirs? Why haven't I ever met you before?"

"Ach, Finrir. You ask too many questions. This is new?"

"Probably, but it would be helpful to know if you'll be around for the next twenty-four hours. We could use your help," Dylan said. But instead of answering, with a quick flick of his shoulders, Conor transformed. Literally. One second, Dylan was looking at a Knight, and the next he was eye level with two red trimmed dragon feet, the deadly claws fully extended, flexing and rutting up the fancy green fairway.

Dylan looked up… and up. He'd wondered if his first take on the dragon's size had been skewed by his situation and the shock of being rescued. But that was not the case. This was one big sucker smiling down at him, rather sarcastically.

"Okay, see you around, I guess."

The dragon's head dipped almost in a bow, acknowledging Dylan's words, then Dylan ducked as one huge foot rose and traveling over his head landed just long enough on the other side of him to push off and up into the sky; the dragon's body followed, as if he didn't weigh as much as a loaded semi. Dylan had to admit as he watched the ebony dragon gain altitude, he was pretty damn impressive. He just hoped he'd stick around.

He made his way back to his SUV and turned the key in the ignition but the engine didn't turn over. What the hell? He tried again, got out and checked under the hood but in the end he knew he would have to call someone to give him a lift to Aurora's. He decided on the likely victim. Jack.

# CHAPTER 14

Jack's phone rang as he drove toward Aurora Borealis. He was tempted not to answer it when he saw *Unknown* on the display but accepted the call. He was surprised to find Dylan on the other end of the line. "Sheriff Lang."

"So formal, Jack." Dylan's voice. "Where are you?"

"I'm on my way to Aurora Borealis, Dylan. I was hoping I'd find you there as well."

Dylan's voice was more cheerful than usual, flippant even. "Well, you're in luck. I'm at Enchanted Glen, and I need a lift."

Jack frowned, not able to imagine a reason why the capable investigator would find himself without transportation and even more curious why he would choose to call *him*. And that led him back to how someone like

Dylan could wind up needing a ride. "What happened to your vehicle?" he asked.

Dylan responded with a grunt. "It won't start, and I need to go with you to Aurora's. I've learned a little something about that guy Flambé you met the other night, something… unforeseen."

Obviously a teaser, and it worked. Jack hadn't seen anything surprise the enigmatic Dylan McGuinness since he'd known him, which hadn't been that long but he felt like he knew him pretty well. "I'll be there in five." The phone bleeped, and the call ended as the usually taciturn PI hung up.

Jack ran through the possibilities in his head. Dylan had discovered the warrior was Aretuu, in which case, Jack was in deep shit. Or, maybe Dylan had just seen him shoplifting at the U-pakIt. Deeper still.

He thought about Tempe and how she'd looked when he'd dropped her at Harmony. She'd been pale, her hair, having lost its luster and color, was darkening, and her eyes no longer sparkled. Her words, that 'he'd get what he wished for… a completely ordinary girlfriend' caused fear to strike him like a viper. He used his training to push back because he wouldn't be able to do his job if he gave in to worry. Jack made a silent vow to see her through the next twenty-four hours.

THE INVESTIGATOR LEANED AGAINST THE CLUBHOUSE, typically casual. He never seemed out of place, Jack thought. Maybe that was part of having to fit in to his surroundings when he was undercover to the point that it was second nature; that and making his eight foot Sasquatch seem invisible. Dylan's SUV sat nearby, apparently out of commission.

Dylan opened the door and got in. Jack took in Dylan's appearance, the mud and grass streaks on his standard black jeans and t-shirt. There was duckweed adorning the pockets and grass poking out of the neckline, along with a foul odor wafting across the short distance between them.

"Jeez, what happened to you? You look like you drowned in pond sewage and you smell worse. How about rolling down that window?" Dylan complied. "And forget the seatbelt. Just try not to touch anything."

"Yes, mother," Dylan quipped. "You're not half wrong. I nearly drowned in the swamp. I would have if it hadn't been for that character with the swords. Tempe said you met him last night at the ball."

When had Dylan seen Tempe? "Wh—" *Don't ask, Jack.*

"Tempe came by Kat's this morning and I was there. She said your ex showed up and you kicked her out—"

"Like hell!" Jack started, but caught the grin on Dylan's face. "Look, can we call a truce or something? We have a lot on our plates."

"Oh, you just *think*..." Dylan reached for Jack's bottle of water and asked, "Can I have this?"

"Sure," Jack said and watched as Dylan poured some of the water on his t-shirt and wiped his eyes with it. Tempe hadn't mentioned any of this. "So you say this Sept Flambé character saved you? The Dark Knight everyone's calling him."

Dylan let out a laugh that sounded a lot like a giggle. Jack had to be imagining it. "He is that. He was on his way to the golf course."

Jack's mind tried to create a mental picture of the Dark Knight playing a round of golf, using one of those swords as a club. It failed. "Anyway, when Tempe came to see me this morning, she told me about this Knight fellow turning up at the ball and about your ex arriving, and she was about to tell me more when we heard—I'm not sure what to call it—a shriek or a bellow from the swamp. She rode my bike to Montana's and I went to investigate. I still had some of my olfactory senses so I went into the swamp and got up close and personal with the swamp *thang*." She saw Jack's raised brow.

"Not my best move. I'd blacked out after it held me down on the bottom, and would have expired if it hadn't been for the Knight. Conor is his name."

"Conor. How did he rescue you from this unseen monster in the swamp? How do you know you weren't having some kind of hallucination?" Jack scoffed.

Dylan clucked his tongue, and got that *I can't wait to tell you this* expression on his face, then blurted, "He's a dragon!"

"A what?"

Dylan grinned, obviously enjoying being the bearer of this news. "And not just any little ol' dragon... no, we're talkin' black, fire-breathing, forty feet tall, teeth like curved swords..." his eyes darted to the side and his eyes narrowed, "...maybe that's where they go."

Jack waited while Dylan had this short conversation with himself and then continued, "Fire shot out of his nostrils... I'm not kidding, Jack. Scared the shit outta me, but that was after he'd plunged his snout into the water and bumped aside whatever was holding me on the bottom and plucked me out of there like a damned crane. Then he unceremoniously tossed me on the bank. It was better than being eaten, I suppose."

Jack contemplated Dylan's story, and asked, "Do they... eat humans?" *Please God, no. That would be more than I could handle.* Yes, he was sure of it.

"This one doesn't apparently," Dylan sighed and put his head back on the headrest while Jack steered the car out of the parking lot. "Or maybe he wasn't in the mood for a low-fat, tough chew like me. So where was I?"

"You mean there's more?" To his own ears, Jack was starting to sound like a tired escapee from a refugee camp.

"He got the news about Lancelot escaping from LSU. Oh, you didn't know. Don't ask me, maybe it's some kind of inner dragon thing like the Pomeroys have, or the *dragon social network,*" he snickered, and Jack mentally recorded another symptom to his list.

"So, he was headed *over...*" Dylan's eyebrows waggled and he flapped his hands to illustrate. Jack rolled his eyes. "...to Enchanted Glen when he spotted my predicament. Afterwards, I drove him to the golf course."

Dylan's eyebrows went up at Jack's expression, "Don't look at me. It was either that or let him *fly* there in broad daylight. Anyway, when we got to the golf course, there was this rather large dude in the middle of the fairway, several holes away from the slew. Conor said the man's name was Garric, we know him as Lancelot." He waited for Jack's reaction. "Yep."

"If I weren't seeing and smelling you while you tell this story, Dylan, I'd think you were under the influence," Jack said, while Dylan just grinned like the star of his own comedy show. He'd never seen Dylan smile like that, like this was all some big joke. It confirmed what he'd told Tempe. Dylan's personality had been affected.

"Wait, Dylan. You said fire-breathing?" Jack thought about the path of fire down the wall at the Bentsons' home and the scorched remains next to the abused victim. He made himself relax, dropping his shoulders. Just as he'd thought—being the Sheriff of a supernatural community wasn't all that different from that of a human community. It was still about collecting evidence, sorting clues and bringing down bad guys.

He hoped.

# CHAPTER 15

Aurora Boreal, the vibrant, clear-headed shop owner Jack was used to, had disappeared. Aurora's hair was almost totally white. To be more accurate, it was a light yellowish gray, which matched her wrinkled skin. As she made her way around the workroom, it was with stiff disjointed movements as if she were in pain.

The change in Aurora's appearance was more dramatic than the others. At least Dylan and Montana still looked like themselves. Maybe shifters were different. Hell, each one of them appeared to be reacting differently to the power down. He didn't even know what Aurora was exactly—a seer, sorceress, witch? Wizardress?

Jack looked at his watch. 11:30 a.m.

Dylan said, "In case I didn't remember to tell you this morning, I didn't like how things went down today with you and Tempe. Where's the ex now?"

The guilt Jack felt had him checking his temper. His voice was calm and his gaze on Dylan direct when he said, "I don't care where she is as long as she stays away from everyone I love." Let him take *that* and smoke it.

"My priority at the time was to get to Jordie before G found her. I left the faerie dog on guard duty at the house in case she comes back, so..." he included Aurora... "let's talk about the Chaos. I know the two moons are coinciding and one will eclipse the other... but I thought everyone was supposed to get stronger as it approached."

Aurora said, rather sniffily, "As I said on *numerous* occasions, Jack. The only thing *predictable* about the Paramoon, which is *synonymous* with *coincidence*, is the fact that it's *imminent*."

*Okay...* Aurora seemed to have turned into a snobby blue-hair, looking down her nose at him and punctuating the bigger words as if Jack needed extra emphasis to understand.

She continued, "I wasn't even aware it was going to happen this month until about three weeks ago. As soon as Cache, the larger magical moon, begins to eclipse the lunar moon, meaning one edge crosses the edge of the other, our powers begin to diminish and all other effects begin. We won't experience the full force of it until it peaks."

Jack's brow rose as he took in the totality of Aurora's condition. How "sick" could she (and Tempe) get?

"Pardon me for stating the obvious, but it seems like you're powerless now."

"Go ahead and say it, Jack," said Aurora. "I look wretchedly old. Thank the gods it lasts only twenty-four hours. We aren't completely powerless, but by the time Cache eclipses Luna tonight, Paramortals who are bound to the oath by blood will be as close to human as they can be, probably weaker."

"Would you explain what you mean by the 'oath' and 'bound by blood'?"

She sighed. Again, there was annoyance at having to explain the details to a *mere* human. Or maybe it was more than that: frustration at having to rely on a human to get them out of this mess, and believing that he couldn't get it done. *We'll see about that.*

"Think of it like this. The oath is the moral component or agreement to stand for the cause, to put one's life on the line for those who are defenseless. The pact, whether by blood or spell, is the *compunction* to defend. Those who inherited the bond through blood will lose their power. This would be Tempestaeries, weres, Dinnshenchas, etc."

"What about vampires? Montana said she's part vampire," Jack said.

Dylan said, "Vamps are a different. Paramortals who are part vampire are bound by the Oath of their hereditary nature. Montana's vamp side will give her strength, but is only bound by her moral obligation to uphold the mission of the Paramortals. Her blood bond will disappear but because the vampire she was bitten by took the Oath as well, you can still count on her. See?"

Aurora said, "By comparison, any Paramortal who was bitten by an enemy vampire will probably lose the ability to process the Oath, once they lose their power. They may follow the enemy's direction. You see how it works, the strongest nature will win out during Chaos. None of the Fae will be affected."

Jack nodded, "Okay, I get it. Who else can we count on?"

"Dick Randall," said Dylan glibly.

"Randall? You're kidding. What the hell is he?" Jack asked. He was getting a *compunction* to wipe that stupid grin off Dylan's face.

"He's an ogre."

"That figures. Who else?"

"Marty, the Pomeroys' Imp. He can shift and who knows what else. Then there's Bella and Petre…"

Jack breathed out a sigh. Now they were getting somewhere, the queen and prince of the Fae. "What about the purple skinned guy and the frolicking fairies I saw at their Inn?" he joked. He was getting a pretty good idea of his little band of warriors.

"Don't make fun, Jack. Some of the tiniest Faeries can pack the biggest wallop," Aurora said.

Jack nodded and asked, "What about 003?"

Dylan stiffened and the goofy smile turned off like a light switch. Aurora's brows rose, "What is it Dylan?"

Dylan hesitated but finally admitted, "Katerina wasn't acting like herself this morning. She tried to bite me, and then when Tempe showed up, she turned into… a lion—not just a panther, but a full grown *male* African lion. If Tempe hadn't distracted her, she'd have probably taken my head off with one swipe. How is that possible?"

"Oh, dear," Aurora said.

"You're sure she's Paramortal?" Jack asked.

Aurora nodded, "Yes—"

"Look, Katerina's been hurt," Dylan said, his staunch support of Kat drawing raised eyebrows from Aurora and Jack. In an uncharacteristic gesture, she placed her hand on Dylan's.

"Chaos is never easy, is it Dylan? It sounds like Jack might not be able to count on Katerina for support."

To say the least, Jack thought, feeling empathetic toward Dylan suddenly. When had he become so involved with Kat? And what did Dylan know about Chaos that he wasn't sharing. "Do you know Katerina's background? Where she came from?"

Dylan hunched over the table, sullen. "She was just starting to open up to me when Cache started to move. I know it looks bad, but try not to over-react…" his voice trailed off, as if he knew he was making an unreasonable request. How could anyone not react when faced with a man-eating lion who wasn't herself?

All Jack said was, "Kat's a survivor, Dylan." *And aren't we all*, but that wasn't a guarantee of survival. "Okay, according to Dylan, there might be someone who could be our *Big Bad*, if he plans on sticking around to help us."

Aurora asked, "Who's that?"

Dylan said, "Conor de Sept Flambé.

Aurora's eyes narrowed briefly and Jack asked, "Did you know the Knight before he appeared last night at the ball?"

She shook her head. "Not specifically. Dragons are everywhere, but I had no idea who or what he was until I heard his name."

Jack opened his eyes. He'd closed them to hide his reaction to *dragons are everywhere*, but now he asked, "What do you mean?"

"His last name gave it away. *Sept* for *Kin* or *Clan, and* Flambé for *fire*. And it was pretty obvious when you looked at the dragon wings across his shoulders."

*Pretty obvious to Aurora, who could have said something, not that he'd have believed it, and what could he have done?* Right. "Who's side do you think he's on?"

"Our side," said Dylan. "He didn't have to save me this morning. If you think about it, it was an inconvenience. And we could have easily had one less Paramortal. I guess he could be neutral. What do you think, Aurora?"

Aurora *shrugged* and looked at her lap.

Jack looked at Dylan. *Goofy* was back.

Jack groaned inwardly. The personalities of the Paramortal leaders around him were devolving faster than you could say *dragons are everywhere*, turning into circus clowns and apathetic degenerates.

Jack drummed his fingers on the counter as Dylan flipped his badge over and over on the table. How long would he be able to depend on the Paramortals for guidance, much less help during the power down?

His phone rang. Looking at the screen he read, *911 call*. "I've got to go."

Dylan said, "I want to ride along."

Jack was already striding toward his cruiser.

## CHAPTER 16

THE SKIN ON CONOR'S NECK QUIVERED, HIS SHOULDERS bunching as he watched the scene on the street in front of him. The Dinnshencha had told him she had a "day job" caring for the sick, in one of the boxy looking medical vehicles with the red lights. He'd searched the streets of Destiny for the last hour, looking for her, which had taken him longer than usual since he couldn't search from the sky. But finally he'd spotted her, and the one she was "caring for".

The man was sitting on the side nearest Conor behind the turning wheel. All he could make out from his angle near the cafe on wheels labeled, *Crawlin' Cajun Mudbugs*, was her thick blue-black mane brushing the man's shirt. The man laughed. Conor's eyes narrowed. He didna' sound ill at all.

He thought he heard Montana say something and the man said, "Watch your teeth, darlin'." A low growl escaped Conor's throat before he could contain it. Montana's head bobbed up but he wasn't able to make out her face, only the back of her head.

The more he watched, the more he was sure that this was no emergency rescue, even in the style of his time, but an amorous liaison between the two partners. Conor's tatts swelled, heat accumulated in his lower body and bubbled up into his nasal cavity. He swore.

"It's Conor, isn't it?" a voice from behind him said carefully. He whirled, his swords slicing the air as the man stumbled back and caught the silver edge of a car to keep from falling to the ground. Conor had barely managed to avoid decapitating the sheriff.

No one ever slipped up on a dragon Knight. *Which spoke louder than anything of how much this Dinnshencha had affected him*. He sheathed the swords while the man straightened. Conor looked back over his shoulder at the medical van.

Vict—Montana's head had disappeared from view and the man had leaned back against the headrest, one hand continuing to fondle her hair and… Conor didn't care what else. His eyes flared briefly as he gathered his wits and turned back to the cop.

"You are the sheriff of this village."

The Finrir—McGuinness—stepped out from the shadows, as the green-eyed man squinted at him, and scratched his head. Conor nodded formally, "I am de Sept Flambé Knight—"

"—of his majesty's realm. Right," said Jack. "I was curious about that, but right now I have a 911 call. I'm Jack Lang, the 'sheriff of the village'," he said with a grin. "If you'll stick around…" but Conor didn't wait for him to finish.

"I'm done here," he said, scowling, and with one look over his shoulder at the window where he'd last seen Montana, he brushed by Jack and stomped away, the heavy metal boots creating a rhythmic *clank, clank* as he rounded the nearest corner.

"Nice to meet you, too," Jack muttered, watching as the disgruntled Flambé stalked away. He didn't look like a dragon in the least.

He looked at Dylan again. For all he knew, Dylan had been seeing things. Flambé was certainly stout enough to save Dylan from drowning as he was.

Dylan said, "What?"

"Nothing. I didn't even get a chance to plead my case with him."

"Yeah, he's bad about leaving in the middle of a conversation."

Jack said, "Wait here while I check out the situation with Montana and Rafe."

Jack walked toward the ambulance. Peggy had called when he was leaving Aurora's and explained that

LIVIA QUINN

Montana's partner, Rafe had called in the 911. He'd requested that Jack personally respond to their 'distress.' Peggy told him they were on post in the ambulance but when he asked, 'Where's the scene?' she'd chuckled on the other end and responded, 'They aren't *at* a scene, Sheriff. They *are* the scene.'

He told her to give Rafe an ETA of five minutes. A few minutes later he'd pulled into the truck stop. Rafe waved at him and then he'd caught sight of the Knight standing by the food truck. At first, he didn't see Montana. His gaze had gone from the ambulance to the Knight and back again. *There.* Montana's head bobbed up into view and disappeared, in the vicinity of Rafe's lap.

*Okay...* he imagined things could get pretty boring sitting in an ambulance for hours on end. He looked back at Flambé. What was his problem? He'd watched for another minute and realized that the warrior was watching for Montana. Each time her hair rose to the level of the window ledge, Conor stiffened, and those blades seemed to vibrate. Curious.

He'd decided he might as well take the bull by the horns, or the Knight by the swords, so to speak and find out what he was about. It hadn't worked out that way, but he'd come away with his head, so he counted that a step forward.

After the Knight disappeared around the corner of the building, Jack approached the ambulance. "Rafe, what seems to be the problem."

A muffled voice said, "Opn vhdmrrr!" Rafe grinned at Jack.

Jack stuck his head in through the window to find Montana's head of thick black hair spilling over Rafe's lap. "Nice to see you again, Montana."

"Phup ru shrwf."

Rafe and Jack laughed, then Rafe yelped. "Damn it, Montana. That hurt."

She let him know how much she cared by searching the floor with her right hand and picking up a huge needle and aiming it in his direction.

"Hrgrrfne".

"We're working on it, Darlin'," Rafe said. Eyes flaring with pain he mouthed 'help' at Jack.

"I've never been called to perform a blow—"

"Bzsntwyuuthk." More jibberish from Montana. Rafe translated, "It's not what you think." Again, he smirked. Regardless of the blood, pain or discomfort, he was enjoying himself.

"Okay, what's the exact nature of the problem, here? I need to see the... uh... landscape a little better." He pulled a flashlight from his belt, "Do you mind?"

"Whatever, man," Rafe gritted through his teeth.

"Hrrrhy," Montana growled.

Jack carefully moved Montana's hair aside to see what

had her locked in the indelicate position. He was shocked to see so much blood on Rafe's pants and on the side of Montana's cheek. She couldn't seem to move her face from Rafe's groin. "I can't see the wound, but that must hurt."

"You don't know the half of it," Rafe muttered. "Her hair is trapped somewhere. I can't see to get it out of my zipper and I'm not crazy about getting my privates zipped along with it. She wanted me to just pull her hair out, but I told her I'd call you before I'd snatch her hair from her scalp."

"Itdushh dt," Montana grunted again, using her head to punctuate.

"Oww. Damn it, Montana, hold still."

Her hand rose to her scalp, but Rafe managed to get his fingers over hers to keep her from following through. "You'll be loose soon." Another fierce mumble came from his lap, and Rafe grit his teeth. Jack winced. "I tried to get my knife in the glove compartment, but I couldn't move in either direction. And Montana can only see one thing."

"Roger that," Jack grinned.

Shining the light around Rafe and Montana, Jack found the problem. In addition to the hair stuck in Rafe's zipper, a chunk of the thick mass had spilled between a worn place in the leather and latched onto a spring under Rafe's seat. She was locked into position. "I found it. Do you want me to try to get it loose—"

"Chtut!"

"She said—" Jack didn't need an interpreter. He cut the hair loose from the seat, giving Montana some freedom of movement but not enough. Rafe eyed his zipper where Montana's hair remained caught.

Jack held up his knife. "Do you want me to...?" Jack asked.

"Not unless it's really an emergency," Rafe said. "Give me the knife." Jack aimed the light for Rafe as he worked at the zipper, while she sent out muffled snarls that caused shivers to run down Jack's spine.

A hand dropped on Jack's shoulder and Dylan poked his head through the window next to Jack's. "Whatup, Rafe? Yow. Now that's what I call *out of service*." He laughed.

Rafe gave Dylan a hard look, then asked Jack. "Is he on something?"

Jack gave a quick shake of his head. "Ignore him."

Rafe nodded, "Hold still, Montana. I'm going to have to cut your hair out of my zipper."

"Gr-phrt..." came the retort.

Ever the gentleman, Jack turned, tugging a complaining Dylan out of the window. "I wanted to watch." Jack pushed Dylan ahead of him toward the car.

"Thank the gods and Sheriff Lang," Montana said behind him.

Jack called out, "Glad I could help."

He heard a door open and turned. Montana was standing next to him. Damn, she was quiet, and fast.

"Thank you, Jack. I mean it. I appreciate you coming…" she grinned. "I mean, tending to this personally. I was very close to his femoral. "

"Yeah, right, whatever you say, Montana." She wasn't joking. "Uh, so that's what you meant when you said you had the feeding thing taken care of?"

"Yes, it was supposed to be a simple blood donation. Rafe has helped me out before—"

"I'll bet—" Jack grinned.

Montana rolled her eyes. "Men. It's not like I suck him dry. He reaps some benefits from it."

Jack threw up his hands. "I don't need details… but you should find a washcloth." He winced.

Her grin died when he said, "The Dark Knight was here when we drove up. If I had to guess, he wasn't in on your relationship with Rafe. He didn't seem to be getting the big picture."

Her lips thinned and black brows angled down over those cobalt eyes. She nodded thoughtfully.

Dylan walked up, grinning at Montana. "So, you and the Knight, eh?" He rubbed his fingers on both sides of his mouth and teased," You probably want to wipe that blood off your mouth before you go lookin' for 'Conor'.

He frowned at her, scratching his jaw. "Don't you find him a bit… terrifying?"

Montana's head angled bit as she smiled at Dylan, her macabre face at odds with her words, "Oh, I don't know. I think he's kinda cute." Turning back to Jack, she said, "We've got to get cleaned up, and then we're out of here. Thanks, again."

"*Cute…*" Dylan muttered as he got into Jack's cruiser. "Maybe she hasn't seen what I've seen."

Jack thought, *And maybe you were hallucinating.* He offered to take Dylan back to this truck. When they got there, Jack discovered it was simply out of gas. He asked Dylan, because he couldn't conceive of the perpetually prepared PI letting that happen, "Have you ever run out of gas in your life, McGuinness?"

Dylan scratched his jaw, where the swamp muck had dried and crusted. "Once. December 7, 1941. And it wasn't my car. I didn't know the gas gauge wasn't working."

Yep, Jack thought. Blame it on the Para-moon.

CHAPTER 17

Montana wasn't sure what to think. Conor had been at their post, which meant he was looking for *her*. When he'd left that morning he'd been a man of few words. *Few words!* No words. It was hard to think of a thousands year old Knight as timorous. Especially, not a dragon. Not the dragon she'd met at the scene on Saturday. He'd been arrogant, swaggering, *powerful*—she shivered just thinking of how he'd looked. She couldn't wait to see him again in his dragon skin. She must talk him into giving her a ride. She smiled. In the sky.

She identified what she was feeling even though it was completely foreign. She was worried, not insecure exactly, but like a teenage girl with her first boyfriend; Montana was worrying whether she'd messed up. If he was even now making assumptions about her relationship with Rafe, and questioning who had her affections.

Had there ever been a time when she was worried about

what a man thought or felt? *About her affections?* It was nearly impossible for someone of her nature and position to give her trust to a male of any species. She supposed Jack Lang had been the only non-Paramortal to gain her respect, and that had been only recently. She answered her own question with a resounding *Never.*

Maybe it was because with other males she'd always had to fear they wanted to take control, to overpower her, to compete with her once they knew her agenda. Or they would feel affronted because her prime objective was aimed at their gender. But Conor knew her power was dwindling, and instead of taking advantage he'd offered to help her compensate.

She'd never met anyone bigger or badder than him, and yet he didn't try to wield his power over the weak—he was, like his name, a man of honor. She needed to find him and explain about Rafe, so he'd understand, and to keep him from, as Tempe would say, "lopping off her partner's head" due to a misunderstanding.

Where would a visiting dragon Knight go to sulk? She didn't have a clue. Destiny had no mountains where he could perch and brood. No willing virgins—just wait, that would change, but hopefully they wouldn't be sacrificing themselves as dragon food like ancient texts suggested because she'd have to fight him in that case. Maybe the best Scotch whisky in town would lure him.

Every time Montana pushed through the swinging doors at Bon Amis she felt like the bad gunslinger from her favorite movie. Liam set a glass of beer in front of her, gave her an odd look, and asked, "Did ye hear about the new lass in town?"

"No, who's that?" Montana looked around at the main restaurant area and then back at the bar. Bailey was waiting on tables but the restaurant didn't appear to be too busy, just a few parties ordering food and two customers at the bar sipping their beers.

Liam leaned forward, "Word is... tis Jack Lang's wife. Least that's how she tells it."

"Jack's divorced. Remember, it was in the news when he ran for sheriff last year."

"Och, I didn't pay any attention. So she's lyin' is she? Well, it wouldn't make Fritz any nevermind." He winked. "Seems he picked her up at the sheriff's house last night and she spent the night wit' him. He thinks he's in love."

"As Tempe would say, *Zeus' holey boxers!* I can't wait to see what Jack says when he finds that out. We were all hoping she'd left. You know, I told Tempe I didn't take out women, but I have a feeling when I meet this one, I may change my mind. If she's bad enough for Fritz..."

Liam nodded. "Yer right as usual, Bran."

Montana gave him the eye.

"Sorry, lass. We've been cousins for too long I guess. It just slipped out."

Bailey set her tray down on the end of the bar and said, "Cousins?" She cocked her head at Montana. "Girl, you're having a really bad hair day." Montana had forgotten about the whack job Rafe had performed but then, it was just hair; it would grow back.

Bailey looked from Liam to her. "I didn't know you and Liam were related." Bailey Duplessis, Destiny's clueless chameleon, leaned against the bar, waiting, oddly attentive. She looked at Liam.

"You need something, dearie?"

"A tourist wants to know what local beers we have."

Liam tapped the bar to indicate laminated list of beers. "Abita—Turbodog, Purple Haze, Strawberry and S.O.S. Don't mention the Andygator. I'm thinkin' I'm out o' it."

"So how are y'all related?"

*Goddess!* It they'd *wanted* Bailey to focus on something they'd have had no luck. Now she suddenly had laser sights? "We had the same, er, uncle," Montana said and Liam crossed his eyes at her above Bailey's shoulder.

Bailey's eyebrows wrinkled and she pursed her lips. "So, that would mean…"

"That we had the same uncle," Montana gritted through her teeth.

She brightened, "Right. Okay." She turned and walked back to her customers.

Liam raised a brow, "Do 'ya think she'll drop it?"

"I think it's already forgotten, Liam. You know Bailey. Very short attention span."

Montana looked around, "Have you seen Katerina?"

"I hav'no," Liam said. "Even though it's overcast and she would normally come around." Katerina had told them when she moved to Destiny that she absolutely could not get out in bright sunlight because her eyes had been damaged and were extremely sensitive, even with the dark sunglasses she wore around the clock.

Montana said, "She must have had extra work to do. Maybe I'll swing by her place later and see how she's faring."

"I wonder what happened to her," Liam said, grabbing a bar towel from the shelf below the bar.

"We'd all like to know. She gets pretty antsy around law enforcement types. I was wondering…"

Bailey placed her tray on the end of the bar in front of Liam. "So, if you two have the same uncle…"

Liam's eyebrows arrowed up and he grinned at Montana as Bailey tried again. "That means your mother…"

"Bailey. Drop it," Montana growled.

Bailey shrugged, "Sheesh, why so touchy?" Montana rose and she said quickly, "It's dropped okay. Everybody is acting so weird. I think I'll try to find my cowboy." Montana relaxed.

"Hey, Montana," one of Liam's regulars at a nearby table called out. "I heard you had a run in with the county badge this morning. Did you pull out your six guns?"

Montana turned to face the man and said, "Who needs guns." Faster than anyone could blink, her hands held two XL tools of her trade. "I've got needles!"

Everyone laughed and some winced at the sight of those monster syringes. "*Holy stickers, Bat-woman*, what do you use those for?" he asked.

"Props." She snickered. "I just happened to have them with me. Liam asked for a couple. Here, Liam."

"Thanks." Liam accepted the syringes and to the burley man he called, "For shooting up my turducken." The sound of the front doors swinging open was followed by total silence and Liam's, "Who the ba-larney blazes is that?"

# CHAPTER 18

LIAM'S JAW DROPPED AS HE REACHED BEHIND THE BAR for his bat.

Montana turned. Filling up the entire doorway with his hulking form, taking in each patron as if to assure himself they were no threat—what a laugh—was Conor in full Knight attire. Montana swore. "You'd think he'd know better than to walk around with those big honking swords on his back. He could cause a panic." Several of Liam's customers suddenly realized they'd forgotten the church picnic or the trip to the grocery store and stampeded out the back door.

"You know this mon?" Liam asked, eyebrows raised at Montana.

Montana turned to what was left of the Sunday crowd, "Don't mind my little brother, folks. He just got his

Mardi Gras costume, and I haven't been able to get him out of it."

Conor's eyebrow rose as she marched over to him, hooked her arm through his and dragged him to the bar, realizing immediately that if he hadn't wanted to follow her, he would have been impossible to budge. "Sit," she ordered.

His eyes flared and she saw a bit of dragon in the angle of his head. *Hmm,* had she gone too far? Then one side of his beautiful lips kicked up, followed by the other until his eyes were alight with humor. Probably hadn't had anyone boss him around in a century or two. She sighed.

"Liam, this is Conor." She pointed from one to the other, "Conor, Liam."

"Those are real swords," Liam pointed out, as if it were a secret.

Conor, ever the verbose chatterbox, said, "Aye."

Montana shot Liam a look but it took him several long seconds to obey, finally busying himself with wiping the counters down and washing glasses, the noise of the water running and clank of dishes allowing Montana to ask her questions. Not that there were many customers around to hear. Most had "escaped with their lives" she was sure she'd read in the Tribune come morning. Or more like *escaped with their limes,* knowing Jane.

Conor had attempted to sit on a bar stool across from Montana, but between his size and the swords, it was impossible and he had opted for leaning casually, or as casually as a deadly swordsman-cum-dragon could lean on the bar of a small town *watering hole*. "This tavern is popular?" he asked looking around.

"It was until you got here. Besides, it's Sunday. Business doesn't—what are you doing here?"

Conor's eyes widened whether at her daring to ask such a question or in surprise because *by gads, he deserved a drink with the best o' them*. As if to make that point, he reached into a hidden pocket and produced a coin, slapping it on the counter in front of Liam with one massive bronze hand. "I'll have a taste of your best, mon, if you please."

Montana corrected, "Liam."

A hint of a smile crinkled the edges of his golden eyes, and he looked over at the bartender, "*Tapadh leat*, Liam." Liam nodded in return. Back to Montana, Conor's brow lifted, *Satisfied?* Liam was taking a closer look at the coin Conor'd given him, biting it with his teeth, then he winked at Montana.

"I asked what you are doing here. I didn't mean at Bon Amis. Why are you in Destiny?" Montana's hands had made it to her hips. It was the pose she struck when she was set on getting answers. Unfortunately, she didn't— deep, down—believe this dragon could be coerced into doing anything he wasn't of a mind to do. Dragons were notoriously stubborn. Or so she'd heard.

Conor took a long gulp of the local beer, S.O.S., and set the glass down on the bar. His eyes lost their smile, and narrowed on her, making her feel like a little bug who was about to be eaten by a big lizard. A really, really big lizard. She willed herself not to shrink back, instead, narrowing hers right back at him defiantly.

He relaxed, lifted his glass in a toast and guzzled the rest. When he'd finished, one bronze finger slid up the side of the frosted glass to collect the cool moisture. His long muscular arm moved toward her gracefully. She watched it, her eyes nearly crossing as his finger met and transferred the droplets to her bottom lip. Involuntarily her tongue flicked out to lick it off.

His eyes swirled and heated. "I saw you earlier, in your medical unit 'caring' for your man," the words low and *almost*...

Her mouth dropped open. Jack and Dylan had told her he was there, but she'd no idea he'd reached this conclusion. "He's—"

"Careful, Victoria. I will know if you lie."

*Really,* Montana's eyes narrowed. *How?*

"Rafe is my partner, *not* my man," she said firmly.

"Looked like you were partners with—how do they say —blessings?" Both black brows sank over those swirling eyes.

"Benefits. And it wasn't what you thought," Montana said, and wondered why she was explaining.

The Knight's handsome face broke into a grin. Which alternately made Montana want to kick him in his metal plated shins or clear off the bar and have him right there. The sword fighting last night had been exciting; for a warrior almost as good as sex, but—who was she kidding—she didn't want to fight with him, not with hands, feet or swords. She wanted him under her. She looked around to see if Liam was listening, then leaned in. His head tilted to match the angle of hers. Curious, he leaned in as well.

She whispered, "I want to ride your dragon."

His chin dropped, both eyes flashed then reduced to gold slits, as they'd done in his dragon form, but the heat receded when he got her true meaning. He grumbled, "This is not a carnival, and I am not your carousel horsey."

Montana waved her hand. "Well, don't get all offended like. I've just been daydreaming about seeing Destiny from the back of a magnificent fire-breathing dragon such as yourself, but..." she shrugged, "...I'm sure you're not the only dragon in the sky."

She willed herself to keep a straight face as tendrils of smoke oozed from his ears and nostrils, escaping in small erratic puffs as if his fire was percolating like Kilauea. His irises changed to the color of orange flame, and the temperature in the bar rose about ten degrees. Her eyes flew open when the tattoos on his back seemed to swell like the molten cap on a volcano before it blows.

She smiled at him mischievously, "You need to lighten up, Conor. Can't you take a joke?"

# CHAPTER 19

MONTANA FOUND HERSELF UPSIDE DOWN OVER TWO VERY wide shoulders sharing the space with those glittering swords, watching rocks skidder away from under his metal boots. *Mother of Zeus,* but he was strong. As her hair flopped against his back she resisted running her hands over the bunching bronze muscles and called over her shoulder, "Um, drago, where are we going?" No response, but his steady march toward… she raised her head to watch the retreating landscape. He was eating up the distance between the bar and wherever he was headed.

To pass the time, she began counting his steps but got bored and gave up. Finally, the road and the trees began to look familiar.

"Conor, where are you taking me?" She wiggled in his grasp, trying to get free.

"Quit, Dinnshencha. You will appear undignified," he growled.

"Well, you're the one who put me in this demeaning position." There was silence on his end for three long strides while he thought about that. "If I had my Dinnshencha power you would not get away with this."

Conor slowed and his broad hands, which had been holding her tightly to him, softened their hold. Moving down her spine, he cupped her butt and lowered her very *very* slowly, until they were eye to eye.

"Which is why we must prepare. And then, tonight..." *Big sigh,* "We will fly, if it is your heart's desire, Victoria."

"Damn it, it's Montana."

"You are much too extraordinary for such an *impuissant* —inadequate—name."

Well, when he put it that way, Montana thought.

"What is your real name, little dragon."

She was sick of the *little dragon* moniker so she steeled herself, breathed it out with a disgusted sigh. "Branislava."

"*Ach, Glorious Protector...* that suits. I get excited just thinking about it."

Montana's eyes widened at the fire leaking from his nostrils. "Well, we'll have to see what we can do about that, fire-breather." She planted her hands around his strong masculine cheeks, felt his jaws flex as he realized her intent. A deep rumble escaped his chest much like the startup of a winter furnace after a hot summer of disuse. Intriguing thought, that. She took his lip between her teeth and tugged, feeling an increase in the heat seeping from his skin. His hands on her butt tightened and he snugged her pelvis tight against his granite-like hardness. It felt like the National Monument, or at the very least the trunk of an oak.

She felt the smile on her face as she anticipated how completely he would fill her, *if* they were suited. Without a gauge from the past to compare, *or* the power that had been a part of her for almost a century, she wondered, and yet, the way he complimented her skills; his respect for other species and for women, his persistence even when he thought she and Rafe were *a thing*; his sheer size and abilities in both forms dazzled her like no other had. She would use *enthralled* but that was a *no-no* word in her occupational handbook for women. It spoke of being under another's spell, without control, which was some-thing she educated her women against—subjugating themselves to a man. Letting themselves become powerless.

Montana had *never* been powerless—well, until now. But the Knight... dragon—whatever, was not really taking advantage of her lack of strength. After all, he had spent hours teaching her the dances that choreographed his own swordplay so that she would survive the chaos. He didn't know about her vampirism. And she didn't yet know him well enough to give up her last secret.

She kept her fangs retracted even though the urge to ingest his rich intoxicating blood was almost more than she could ignore.

He leaned her against the wall of her own home while he drizzled fire down her neck to her breasts, leaving a scorching trail of desire that traveled even further to her core. "Beautiful Branislava, the queen of defenders."

He eased back from her and let her slide down his massive body. That was another thing. She was no petite miss but six feet of muscle and speed, albeit "six luscious feet", remembering something he'd said at her house that morning. With him, she felt almost delicate in size, not weak, as he never made her feel the way the abusers she'd annihilated over the years had made their victims feel. This dragon lived up to his Knight-ness.

"I have watched you from afar." *Hmm, that was probably an exaggeration.* "We will take *each other*, but first, we will practice. You must learn less honorable ways to fight."

"Hey, I can fight dirty—*oww,* what was that for?" She rubbed her butt, and looked up at him from the floor of her concrete porch where she'd landed when he'd dropped her unexpectedly.

"The first lesson in death fighting: Honor has no place. Do not give your opponent a chance to predict your next move. If I'm right, you've had the advantage of surprise in most of your past confrontations, and the ability to shift which you will not have."

She rolled and found herself between his legs as he

LIVIA QUINN

anticipated her. Only pure strength and speed allowed her to pop his knee from behind and roll out as he stumbled. "Very good." He pronounced it *guud*. He reached down to give her a hand, "Shall we go inside?" She took his hand planning to use the momentum to surprise him, but he'd seen that one before—not one of her cleverest ideas, anyway. He flicked his wrist and brought her into him like a top, or one of his dance moves —ballroom?

Wrapped in arms like steel she brought her heel down on his metal boot, which just made him chuckle and tighten his hold until she was incapable of taking a breath. He shifted and her heel caught the soft pad beneath his knee, making him stagger. She leaned to that side and he lost his balance, but her delight was short-lived as his hand tightened on her breast and he kissed her neck.

It was so unexpected, she moaned. He whispered into her skin, "I believe it's time we went inside to continue your training, little dragon."

He pulled the door open as he continued to alternate kisses and fire down her throat. She moaned again. His hold loosened so he could set her feet on the floor of her great room. She bent over, pretending to get her breath. His hand rested on her back.

"Did I hurt yuu—oomph!" He tumbled to his back. She leaped across the expanse of floor and reached for Mathilda, her hand clasping the hilt tightly, then with a dive away from his previous position and an acrobatic

146

flip, she landed, sword at the ready. *He* had only drawn one sword and with it he swatted hers away as he kicked her foot out from under her; her head cracked on the tile floor, and she came nose tip to sword tip with 'Excalibur' or whatever he called his sword.

She blinked his image into focus. So far he hadn't done anything that a common street fighter couldn't have thwarted. He was right; she was weaker and needed some new moves if she was going to be able to overcome the loss of her Dinnshencha power.

He helped her up, the iron strength of his arm making her want to get to the *taking each other* part now, rather than later. "A warm up to start. Remember the minuet? Its beat is delicate, even, precise. Let's review the basics, like this."

He demonstrated, humming the melody while he corrected her style, admonishing her to *"balance, get your weight centered between 'those heavy feet'. Light—like the music— inhale quietly, turn, thrust. "Now the new moves I showed you, feel the rhythm."*

Sooner than she expected their warm-up ended and Conor stood over her, swords sheathed once again, "Close the curtains." Balancing on one foot, he removed one boot dropping it to the floor with a heavy *clunk*. The other followed.

*Huh?* Practice was over and now he wanted payment?

# CHAPTER 20

"THAT WAS HARDLY WORTH A KISS MUCH LESS SEX," Montana said.

He actually snickered. "Tha' twas *hardly* a kiss, and we hav'nae begun to train. Dinna be so impatient, Branislava. We'll get to the love-making, and you will nae be disappointed, eh?"

She'd known he was arrogant but she felt a silent eye-roll nevertheless. "We need complete darkness," he said, prompting her once again.

Montana did as he asked while he closed the other shutters to block out all filtered light. When she pulled the curtains on the last window and turned, the room was black and the Knight blended as if he didn't exist. She assumed she did as well.

She listened for movement. There was none. Gripping Mathilda with her right hand, she searched the darkness for some hint, a lack, a movement with her left. She sensed his heat first approaching from her right.

"Aye, use all your senses," his voice came, low and from all directions. She swung her sword to the right. "Close your eyes," his voice whispered, from somewhere else. How did he do that? She inhaled—"*Don't*. Make your breathing invisible. Your opponent should'nae be able to see or hear your breath. T'will give away your next move."

She exhaled, allowing the breath to mingle with the air around her slowly. "*Ach*, stop concentrating so hard. I can hear your brain. Center yourself as *if* you had your power. Allow your natural abilities and senses to take over for what you have lost."

She slid silently to her left, inviting her senses to do the work her eyes could not. *There*, a wisp of air, her blade came up and clashed with Conor's, slid along its length as she spun and crouched, exhaling a controlled breath and a slow silent intake. There it was again, this time she was sure it was a step, and his heat. Her leg came out parallel to the ground and swiped, hearing his grunt as he leaped and hit the floor on the other side of her.

"Good. Now stand, extend the sword in front of you," he said. Matilda's edge touched his blade and as he slid it along the length of hers, she heard him start to hum. *The songs from the dance.*

With the moves he'd taught her, now, she would fight him in the dark. The first of her strikes was awkward.

His baritone tune paused, "Keep your weight balanced", and resumed as he walked through the steps with her in the dark. *Hmm hmm hm, Mm-mmm, satisfaction." Move, turn, lunge, strike-slide-free, parry, spin, strike... "I can't get no-o..." Lunge retreat spin-out, duck.* She recognized the tune as the beat set the pace for each of the moves; she turned and parried, found her rhythm and realized she was *seeing* through her other senses.

She heard his breath, felt the heat of it, and the scent of his skin suddenly seemed a part of her. When his back was to hers she slammed the sword hilt into his shoulder, the loud clank of one sword confirmed her aim, but no exhalation, no cry of pain. He was good. Silently, she made three crouched turns in a direction she thought was away from him, rose quietly just as both of his arms manacled her upper body and he whispered, "You're dead, little dragon."

"DAMN." HER SHOULDERS DROOPED AS HE LOWERED HIS head to her neck again and ran a lick of fire along it. She knew it was his fire, but why didn't it burn? "I guess I flunked, huh?"

He chuckled against her neck. "*Ach*, nae. Ye did fine. It was black as pitch, ye ken?" He released her and walked to the front windows, spreading the curtains wide.

"You could see... in the dark," she accused. "That wasn't fair."

"*Ach*, remember my first point. You must never think

about fair when you fight to win. Only strike first and fast, and repeat 'til your opponent is dead. Now, *again*, and stop holding back. You must practice as if you fight to the death."

Those were the words she needed to hear. There was no other being she could practice with *'to the death'* without fear of harm. She assumed Conor would be able to turn away or fend off any attack by her, but he'd ordered her to fight him to the death so she would be prepared for anything up to his level. Her heart did a giant flip. He was *seriously* awesome. *And now back to the fight, Montana.*

His golden eyes narrowed as he looked into hers and said, "Always assume a friend *could* be your enemy." He drew both swords this time and she jumped back, hiding her surprise, doing two backflips to gain some time to set her own sword, as he began to sing this time, in a beautiful rich baritone, "I can't get no... satisfaction. *Unh, two, three,* and... I can't—fight, damn you!"

So, she did. Back to back they moved, trading blows, feet and hands moving to his choreography, with his voice droning on. Her movements became more fluid, her breathing quiet and sure, her strokes more responsive than ever which sent her confidence soaring, until he whipped his swords in his classic scissor move and caught her between them. "More."

He spun away and this time she recognized the beat of "Battle Cry" with its ethereal beginning, the smooth kata like movements and Conor's voice, "No one can save you now... do or die", then he performed a back-

151

flip, his feet landing against the door, kicking it open as he rolled through, continuing the artful twin-blade exhibition while she stood gaping. He landed to the imaginary pause in the violins and gave her a gesture to join him.

She strode through the arched doorway and into the clearing, which was coated in a light dusting of snow, though around his feet it was melted. She attacked, leaping into the air and bringing her blade down on his, then in a side twist, landed to his left and ducked as his other sword whistled over her head.

She felt the throbbing beat in her blood and lunged. He parried. She thrust. He countered, and on it went until the last seconds of the silent music died, a battle cry on her lips as his blade clashed with hers. He said, "Well done."

She lowered Mathilda and turned away. He circled her neck with his arm and pulled her back to him. "I said, assume yer friend could be your enemy, Branislava. Never turn your back. Never, on *anyone*. Never let your guard down unless your back is resting against a wall; and then remember, some beings can rip off roofs and burn through walls."

She got it. Montana nodded, and tossed her sword across the clearing. She felt his hard erection pressing into the small of her back, moved her hips against him, raised her arms to feel the steel over satin biceps. He was hard all over, and she meant to have him right now. No more fighting, no more talking, no more dancing, just…

her lips tilted up in a smile... *satisfaction*. She would *get some.*

His broad palm came up to cup her cheek turning her face up to his. Dark eyes stared into hers, simmering with inner fire. "You are a clever woman and an exceptional fighter even though you are down to mere human strength. I fear you may not be clever enough to surprise a truly fearsome being, though, little dragon. I worry for you."

"I've lived nearly a century without your training, Knight, not that I don't appreciate it. I realize my Dinnshencha power has been more... automatic... less instinctive."

"I see *some* improvement—" his brow rose beneath his lush black hair.

"Gods, but you're hard to convince. But then, you're just *hard.*" She wiggled against him again and this time he groaned, or growled, she wasn't sure what to call the sound emanating from deep within him, but she felt it all the way down her spine. Her hands roamed down his powerful hips, up his arms to stroke his biceps. He turned her and took her mouth in an explosive kiss, one that sent heat skidding through her blood and turned her limbs to liquid fire.

He muttered into her ear. "So fierce, so proud..."

"So annoyed, Conor. Shut up and kiss me." She gripped his hair in her hand and dragged his head down to hers.

# CHAPTER 21

PLEASURE POOLED IN HER BELLY AS HIS MOUTH CAME back down on hers. She loved the fact that he was romantic and wanted to list her attributes; she liked his as well, but there was a time for talk and this wasn't it. She pulled on his hair to bring him closer, devoured his mouth with hers, sucked on his tongue while her hand roamed over his granite length, stroking his skin until she felt fire oozing along her cheek. Her hand went to her cheek reflexively, feeling for a burn and found it cool to the touch.

She drew back to look at him. His irises were a fiery orange, the tiny stream of fire that trickled from his nostrils wound down her neck. She followed its path as it sizzled its way along the front of her shirt, circled her nipples, lighting up the nerves to her center. His tongue teased her bottom lip and plunged in to dual with hers.

Her eyes closed as he scooped her up, deepening the kiss

and striding across the lawn for the woods. She looked up at him quizzically. "More room," he said succinctly, then he set her down on the wide sawed-off trunk of an ancient cypress and started removing his swords.

She was naked before he'd ditched the swords, because when it came to the Dark Knight, she didn't want to miss a thing. He smiled seductively, much like a male burlesque dancer might do to entice more tips, then he untied one leather strip from his brawny arm. Thinking he would move to the next arm, she watched curiously as he reached for his belt and dropped it beside him with a *clink*. Next went the wrist guards, a boot, the other leather strip…

The flex of his biceps made her stomach grip with lust, but when he dropped those strange silky gauchos, her breathing hitched and she felt herself go wet.

"Mother of Zeus, Conor, but you are beautiful." He stood, a statue of an ancient conqueror as she approached, placed both hands on his chest, stroked the length of his torso, absorbing his heat. He really was like a giant furnace, with heat emanating from every pore.

Her hands itched to feel the black leathery skin on his wide muscled shoulders. Under her fingers they felt surprisingly soft, like the way snakeskin was slick and pliable, not wet or rough like you expected. They fluttered a bit at her ministrations and she guessed it was a sensual quiver, since his pecs jumped as well.

Something bounced against her belly and she looked

down. He was long and thick, and waiting patiently for her to finish exploring. But she was far from finished. Her hands grasped his wrists, though her fingers could only fit around half the circumference. He allowed her hands to travel over him.

Watching his face as the flames leaped in his eyes, she trailed her fingertips across the massive width of his hand, bumped over his knuckles, reached under them and lifted, joining her fingers with his. His arms were heavy so he held them aloft where she placed them and smiled as she moved in closer, rubbing her lower body against him, dragging her nipples against his torso, across his hot smooth skin.

She closed her eyes, inhaling his scent, feeling his desire as a low hum of vibration, then as a growl rumbling up from a deep well. Powerful arms plucked her from the ground as if she were a slender nymph and carried her to a lush grassy place beneath some thick cedars. Lowering her to the ground with one arm, he followed, his black hair flowing around her head as he devoured her mouth with a kiss meant to claim.

His unique scent surrounded her as their tongues tangled like mating snakes and their bodies responded to the urge to complete the love play their mouths enacted. A wide splayed hand dragged down her toned stomach to dip into the wet crevice below. His lips left her mouth and drew a path down her throat with fiery hot kisses, to her chest, laving her nipples, navel, and lower.

CONOR SPREAD HER LEGS SO HE COULD DIP INTO THE honeyed sweetness of her juices. She was ready for him but he intended to take his pleasure only after he sent her to the stars. She was not one to relinquish control and he reveled in her trust, in the way her limbs went limp before him, allowing him to simply feast on her, sipping at her core, suckling her nipples while she writhed with pleasure and encouraged him assertively.

He smiled at her crude commands, a warrior through and through was his Branislava. He spoke her name reverently just to watch her eyes flare with irritation. "But you're glorious, love. You cannae deny your name. This 'Montana' is still within you but I'm loving the warrior, the defender at the heart of your strength."

Her breathing increased and Conor drove one finger into her as he kissed the bud protected within the swollen petals at her center. As her back arched she cried out, and screamed his name. He lifted her into his hands and spun toward the trunk of the nearest tree, plunging up deep inside her as she throbbed around him, squeezing him tightly and taking him deeper with every driving thrust. He plowed her receptive heat until she was panting his name, begging him not to stop. He didn't want to, but *Gods* it was too good. She was too tight, and it was meant to be now.

He roared as he reached new territory, as it were, some-where neither had been before, not just a physical summit but a wellspring of feelings based on mores, history, passion, practices and common purpose. A smile curved his lips.

If he told her he'd never experienced such in thousands of years, she would probably not let him touch her again. He walked with her legs wrapped around him, her head against his shoulder, arms limp at her sides.

Well, at least there was that, he thought. Then, she stirred.

# CHAPTER 22

Conor's large hand splayed gently across Montana's back as he sat on the ground, the large shaft inside her coming to life once again and pushing into her. He plucked her arms from her sides and pulled her across him to gaze into her eyes.

*There* was that smug, I'm-the-baddest-dragon-on-the-block look again. Well, she'd give him that. She'd never felt more fulfilled by a lover before. She'd wanted to believe it had been just a matching of needs, purely sexual compatibility because of what they shared... but was there more to it?

She ran her tongue across that wide smiling bottom lip and tugged it into her mouth as she angled her hips into his taking him deeper. Then she raised her arms above her head, lifted her hair, thrust her breasts up toward him, and watched his eyes change again, taking on that orangy color she knew meant he was *on fire* for her.

She moved her hips seductively, angling from alternating directions until he groaned and pushed up into her. Then lowering her hands to his rock hard abdomen, she *rode the dragon,* hard and fast.

She pushed him, met each of his upward thrusts with a plunge of her own, taking him so deep it was a wonder he didn't carve her in two. And then light splintered in a thousands shards of fiery sparks, her vision going dim as she closed her eyes briefly to savor the pleasure unlike ever before.

When she opened them, there was no longer a smug expression on his face, but one of such intense bonding and confidence, it made her nervous to contemplate it. He let her slide off but caught her before she could stand and pulled her down to him, cuddling her in the snow, his natural heat keeping her nice and toasty.

Trying to distract him because this was getting *way* too… cosy, she said, "You never did tell me why you're here. And don't give me a line about being here to show me your moves. I've seen them, and you're still here."

"I am charged with watching over a new Paramortal."

A new Paramortal. "Tempe?" or Jordie…With his head resting on one massive bicep, he moved it back and forth. "Okay keep your secret, but what about this weakness you mentioned to me earlier?"

He chuckled and she felt the reverberation through her back, "I have only one, and luckily it's nae been an issue, because I wouldnae be in combat with one whom I'd been loving."

"*Ahh,*" she said, rolling up, with sudden inspiration.

"I have a question though," he asked.

She waited. He looked like he was embarrassed. "What's a... mudbug?"

Montana laughed. "It's not what you'd think. Simply a small crustacean folks around here eat. They crawl out of the mud in the winter and spring."

"*Ach,* I thought t'was some fearsome enemy I'd not heard of."

Montana said, "How about you tweak my hand-to-hand skills, drago?"

He grunted. "I dislike this word '*drago*'. It is slander?" He set her free and rose while she stretched taking a stance opposite him. He cocked his head awaiting an answer, running his eyes over her.

"Think of it as a pet name," Montana said, flexing her neck from side to side and swinging her arms. He frowned down at her as his eyes tracked to her bouncing breasts, his cock rising once again. "Conor, what you need is a good fight. The winner gets a reward," she teased, getting the reaction she expected, the lifted brow, and the sexy confidence.

"*Ach,* well then, you should simply come here and let me take my bounty."

"*Uh-uh.* Let's work to my choice of music this time, a song by a young entertainer who has made a big difference to many of my young women. Last year she performed for the girls at my Destiny shelter. She's someone they can aspire to be, to overcome their present circumstances. In any age, she would have been an advocator for women, ahead of her time."

She started humming as she moved step over step in a circle around him. He watched her, and one careful step after another got into the rhythm, as she sang, "I knew you were trouble when you walked in," *sidearm, chop, counter,* "…you took me to places I've never been…" *spin, chop, duck, punch.*

He grinned and got into the fight, neatly turning her blows, striking her in the side, but not with all his might, *the damned chicken.* She'd show him. "Fight, Conor. I'm not some novice off the volunteer draft line." She pounded her chest and nearly burst out laughing when his eyes widened on her breasts. "I am Dinnshencha. I *will* defeat you."

*Hah, that got through.* His speed increased as she sang, the song's lively rhythm setting a challenging pace. Moves matched beats, her breathing increased but she controlled it. She met his chop with her forearm, spun and ducked, punched. He twirled. It was a beautiful movement on one leg and his nakedness merely put each muscle and tendon into their best light as he lifted off the ground, shifted into dragon form and landed beside her as if to say, *What will the Dinnshencha do with this?*

She looked up into that smug expression, remembering his earlier words as she stood nearly eye to eye with his dragon danglies, and without telegraphing, smiling, breathing or in any way announcing her next move, she struck, nailing the large but tender dragonly parts with two rapid blows.

At first, nothing happened. Then an unpleasant malodorous smoke blew out of his snout and his head teetered on his neck like a bobble-headed dragon toy. His back bowed, shoulders drooped, and his long neck whipped around in an arc. Montana scampered back; he was going down. She yelled, "Conor, wake up!" He just groaned, and the sound was horrible.

His giant head rolled to the right and knees shaking, he sagged. His wings clipped the limbs off the cypress trees and then all forty-feet of fierce, *invincible* dragon spiraled to the ground with a shuddering crash, rocking Montana down onto her knees. The massive mountain of black scales took in a long shuddering breath, and let out a painful rasp.

*The bigger they are… the harder they fall.* She smiled. She just couldn't help it. He had told her he was afraid she wouldn't be able to take down a truly fearsome being, *like him*. She felt *somewhat* bad because he wouldn't have shared his secret with just anyone. *Ironic, really.* Someone might even say it was a cheap shot. Well, he'd said, "Fight as if to the death", not believing for a minute that she could bring him down. And she hadn't *killed* him, though he might wish she had.

Montana crawled over to him, humming, stroking his handsome horned forehead. As one bleary eye the size of her head drifted open, she sang, "Now you're lying on the cold, cold ground."

The eye closed and a very big wheeze escaped him. *Aww.* She watched him until he started to change back. It took longer this time.

When he was once again a naked Knight, she stroked his human brow, regretting the pain she'd caused him. She thought of the old adage, *This will hurt me more than it hurts you.* Her heart flipped when he sighed and looked up at her.

"You, my precious one, are a devilishly vicious woman." One side of his mouth crooked up in a smile, then he moaned and covered his groin as if fearing she might take another shot. "Twas a lesson bought and paid for. One I shall remember forever."

She lay next to him while he recovered. She could see why he hadn't shared his secret. He'd been laid *very* low, put completely out of commission, not a good thing for someone of his power and size to be that vulnerable. Perhaps she should stay close when he fought, protect his *low* side. But he'd said it wasn't a problem unless he was fighting the one he'd been intimate with. *That* made her feel even worse.

*He shared his secret with you...* her conscience niggled. She sighed and made her decision to share her own secret with him though she might be sorry. How would he feel when he found she was a some-time blood sucker? Many in her past had been disgusted by the knowledge, disdained her and turned away. After what she'd just done, would he still trust her after knowing everything about her?

She propped her head on her hand and the next time he opened his eyes, said, "You may wish you hadn't trained me, once you know *my* secret." She sighed. "Rafe and I have an arrangement, but it's not about sex. He gives me blood." She showed him her fangs. His brows lifted. He stroked her hair away from her face, stared into her eyes with his fathomless black ones and said, "Bite me."

# CHAPTER 23

HER FIRST THOUGHT WAS THAT ONCE AGAIN SHE'D BEEN rejected because of her nature. "Well, that's a helluva note."

Then he turned his face away from her, his big hand reaching up to gather his hair, exposing his strong corded neck. The pulse at his throat marked the vein through which his rich, no doubt, magical blood flowed. She swallowed the lump in her throat and wondered at him through blurry vision. He was one surprise after another. She'd never known a man, or a creature, like him.

The ground would have been icy, but he'd used his breath to create a warm place for her to lay beside him. He could have used his power to terrorize, and strength to overwhelm, but he showed her only tenderness and protection and selfless caring.

And now, in a weakened state with his neck vulnerable and exposed, he offered his very blood, along with his total trust. Their swordplay had been more than instructional; it was passionate and primal. It seemed almost as if her Dinnshencha had found her soul mate.

"Thank you, Conor, but I'll take a raincheck." In answer to his dubious expression, she kissed him. "Let's see what happens tomorrow. I need to send Jack a text about something that happened earlier." She laid her hand against his heart, "I'm sorry I hurt you."

"I'm sorry as well." His eyes glinted with laughter. "It hurt like hell, ye ken? But I have only me'self to blame, Victoria. *Ach*, today, it suits you, so don't protest. That lesson will benefit us both. I'm proud of you. If I *could*," he sighed and winced, "I'd show you how much."

She rolled onto her back and reached for him. He spread her legs gently, ran those big hands reverently, slowly down each "luscious" inch of her body. It turned out he had more in his repertoire than just the *old standards*.

THE SOUND OF THUNDER WOKE TEMPE FROM HER NAP. Blearily she walked to the kitchen window looking for the noise and froze. *Not thunder.* Freddie the *Toolman* had removed the huge sheet of black plastic covering her dining room window and the sight that almost drove her to her knees was accompanied by frigid air and light

167

snow blowing in through the window opening. How could she have slept through the racket of the rented crane and preparations to install the replacement window?

She leaped from the couch intending to call out… to stop him from destroying yet another costly pane, but paused in the opening. Instead of her usual bumbling handyman, Freddie was working the controls like a pro. Who in their right minds had turned Freddie loose with heavy equipment? If he knew how to operate a crane, why didn't he concentrate on that, rather than piddling with fixit tasks he inevitably screwed up?

He pointed to the man holding the edge of the large windowpane and shouted at him, "We're going straight in, just don't let go of that corner. This window is going to be installed without a hitch this time or my name isn't Freddie Taylor."

Tempe smiled. She'd better change and get out there before things went South again, she thought, even though Freddie seemed to be making all the right choices.

She was still dressed in the storm gray ball gown. She surveyed the damage her morning jaunt had done to it. The hem was dirty and a bit ragged but all in all it had survived fairly well. She'd have it cleaned and hemmed and it would suit to box up and pull out twenty years from now to look back on a memorable night.

Even after a long nap, she felt weary, sore, and unhappy.

The soreness was understandable given that she and Jack had spent nearly three hours making love prior to the *rude* arrival of his ex. The weariness , the after-effects of everything that had gone down in the last two weeks, but with the exception of the approaching Chaos, things had turned around. River was safe, she hoped. Jack had explained *G-Crazy*'s arrival and practically begged her to understand. She couldn't put her finger on the problem. Maybe she just needed a good night's sleep.

They all had to be on alert for the next twenty-four hours though, so she'd better double up on the caffeine. What could she do to help? She had no power, and not enough history as a Paramortal to offer much input into their strategies. Maybe that was it—she'd just accepted her part in the community and now… it almost seemed as if she'd lost more than just her Tempestaerie power.

Freddie seemed to be experiencing the opposite. Perhaps the full moon was more enhanced during Para-moon. Aurora or someone would document all the challenges and circumstances brought about by the Coincidence, but what good would it do? The next one might not happen for hundreds of years.

She chose not to distract Freddie by calling out to him while things were going so well. Instead she went to her room and carefully undressed, slipping on a thigh length shift then walked down a level and out onto the back porch. River had suggested extending the rear porch and Tempe had agreed. She loved being able to sit outside no matter the weather, since she was immune to its effects. Or she *had* been, before today.

She shivered, crossing her arms over her chest. Light flurries drifted down from gray skies. Would the thick clouds obscuring the eclipse diminish the effects of the Para-moon? She could only hope. She waited until Freddie saw her and walked in the direction of the rental crane. Freddie cut the engine back so he could hear and directed his helper not to move, in no-nonsense tone. The worker nodded his head and obeyed.

"Ms. Tempe. Now, I need you to step back out of the way so you won't get hurt. In another five minutes we'll have this baby in and you can watch the picture post-card the snow and the full moon are going to make of your backyard through that new window. When I saw the weather moving in and thought about the mess I'd made of your living room wall, I called Dave here and borrowed a crane from Max Rutledge for a few hours. He said to tell you, 'No charge'."

Tempe just nodded at the stranger in front of her. She'd recently laid down the law after his continual screw-ups, denying him access to any projects unless she or River were in charge. But here he was, confident, vocal, capable—was the old Freddie gone for good? "Can I do anything to help?" She shivered again. She'd learned a lot in the remodeling process and could wield a hammer or use a nail gun with the best of 'em.

Freddie shook his head. "Don't bother that pretty—

Tempe, what happened to your hair? It's… I mean, it's not red anymore. I probably shouldn't have mentioned it. We'll just go to back to work so we can get this equipment back to Max."

"Thank you, Freddie. I mean it. River would be proud."

He nodded curtly and reached for the controls. Tempe watched the men as the huge window went seamlessly into place. Freddie was right. She'd missed that view from her living room of the slope down to the Forge. But she couldn't see herself enjoying the view of the Para-moon tonight, knowing what was to come.

Tempe stepped off the porch. An older model Ford truck rumbled to a stop beside the house and Jordie got out of the passenger side. *Shy*, the son of one of Tempe's customers, and the star of the boy's basketball team turned the engine off and joined her.

The first time Tempe had met Shy, he'd come out to take the mail from her in his mother's fuzzy bathrobe and her pink slip-ons. Jarell said a "real man" could wear pink slippers, especially if they were his mama's. After she'd surprised him by knowing his statistics as the team's best shooter, he'd made it a point whenever he was home to fill her in on the team's current news.

Jarell Johnson was a 4.0 student who enthused about his teacher's strategies as if he was hoping take her place someday. Tempe hadn't realized he was Jordie's friend but it made sense, since Jordie was the top player for the girl's team and an honor student as well.

"Hi, Tempe," Jordie waved and hurried to Tempe, hugging her a bit longer than usual. "Did you...uh... have fun at the ball last night?" Jordie asked nervously. "Daddy said he took all my advice, but I wanted to hear it from you." She turned to Shy. "Do you know Jarell?"

Tempe nodded at Jarell, "Shy and I are old friends." She turned back to Jordie, whose smile didn't reach her eyes. "Your dad was the ideal Prince Charming—limo, fancy tux..." she trailed off, not sure if she should mention G's arrival.

Jordie glanced at Jarell. He said, "If y'all don't mind, I'm going to wander down to the bayou." A true Louisianian, he pronounced it 'bah'. He studied Tempe a second too long and said, "Ms. Tempe, you look cold. Why don't you take my jacket while I check out the fishing." He took it off and tossed it to her, the warmth of it nearly making her groan.

She thanked him and said, "I think there's a pole leaning up against the side of the house and there are some jigs in the bait box right there by it." Pretty frosty for a fish to bite, but Shy knew that, so this was about giving Tempe and Jordie time to talk.

"*Allriiight*," the boy grinned and headed in the direction Tempe pointed. "Y'all take your time."

Tempe smiled at Jordie, "Guess he likes to fish. Now what brings you by to see me?"

# CHAPTER 24

JORDIE WATCHED THE WINDOW REPLACEMENT PROCESS for a minute as if she were contemplating taking up contracting. Finally she said, "I heard you met..." her voice hitched. Apparently, neither father nor daughter was inclined to actually name the mother. So Tempe made it easy for her.

"I did. She seemed," *hmm*, what to say...

"Crazy? Overbearing... slutty? Yeah," Jordie exhaled, "don't worry about hurting my feelings. I hate her. Hate. Her." Her voice trembled and she blinked rapidly, turning to watch Jarell walk, pole in hand, toward the swamp.

"He's a great guy." She inhaled unevenly and turned back to Tempe. "We were at basketball practice, and I wanted to talk to you, so Jarell offered to give me a lift. I promised Daddy I'd have him or Andy with me at least if I went anywhere. He's terrified that she'll come back and kidnap me, or something. Like that would be possible. I wouldn't have even answered the door, if I'd been him."

Tempe said, "He didn't know who it was, Sweetie. He was worried you might have forgotten your key."

Jordie looked down the yard toward the swamp to where Jarell had dragged up a five-gallon bucket and was poking around in the bait box for the perfect bait. "He's not going to catch anything you know," Tempe said trying to lighten the moment, but Jordie was somewhere else.

"I know you understand since you and your mom had issues, Tempe, but she wasn't a liar and a thief. My... *mother...*" She said it with so much vehemence, Tempe thought. "She was never ever there for me. My dad has always been *it*, *totally*, mother and father. He was gone a lot but he called, wrote letters, and even managed to get home a couple of times during his tour for special functions like my third grade matriculation. I was in a talent contest that night. My teachers were all in on his surprise. When my performance was over, they announced someone was there to give me my second place ribbon. It was Daddy."

With a tremulous smile she said, "He's the best." She wiped at her eyes and said, "That's why I cut him so much slack. He's been through a lot." Her eyes suddenly were seeing into the past again.

"G is a worthless human being. She had actually been in town for six whole months during that time so I was staying with her, not Granddad and Grandma. When we got home from the school that night she was gone. She'd cleaned out the closet, the bank account, even my little savings account in my piggy bank. She left the pieces of my piggy on the floor as if to say, "Screw you, little girl." Her shoulders dropped and she exhaled with too much fatalism for a teenager. Tempe recognized the emotion.

"What did your father do?" She could only imagine how Jack had reacted.

"Daddy took a month's leave. It took an Act of Congress with his superior,s but because there wasn't a big offensive going on overseas, he worked it out. After that, I stayed with my grandparents when he wasn't home."

Tempe frowned, "Where was G?"

"That time she stayed gone almost two years. It was great. Like being a normal kid, 'ya know? Except I missed my dad." Tempe had never had a chance to be a normal kid but she understood. She'd missed Dutch desperately.

"I'd just started to think she wasn't coming back when up she popped again, looking completely different—the blonde, green contacts, poured into her clothes. It was embarrassing. She kept making a show at being the TV show 'mom' but she stunk at it. My friends just thought she was weird, and when we were alone… I was afraid of her. There's something *wrong* with her."

"What happened?"

"My grandparents went on a cruise after she'd been around for a few months and seemed like she was settled. As soon as they left, she took everything she could and split, again. I was by myself for three days until the Navy guy could get in touch with Daddy. He and my grandparents were all there within two days. You know how you know it's not your fault but you feel guilty anyway?"

"I do," Tempe said, rubbing Jordie's shoulder.

"That's when Daddy hired the private investigator and my grandparents became my temporary guardians until he got out of the service. I don't know what the investigator found out but one day, Daddy showed up and he was shooting daggers. He said, he'd hired a lawyer and was taking her to court for full custody. He promised never to leave me again. And he didn't." Jordie's eyes were sad. "He loved flying—"

Tempe pulled the teenager in for a hug, "He loves you the most, Jordie. It's obvious to everybody who his number one priority is." It was the reason the whole *finding-out-your-little-ordinary-town-is-a-freak-show* thing was so hard to take. "And that's how it should be. The burden shouldn't be on the kid." *Huh.* Someone had told her that recently hadn't they?

"So that's when your dad went to work for the Memphis

Police department?"

"Yeah, you think Destiny's odd…" She frowned. "You look really cold, Tempe. Do you want to go inside?"

Tempe shook her head, gritting her teeth to keep them from chattering. She wanted to hear the rest of this. "Were they divorced then?"

"Yes. Actually, Daddy got an annulment, full custody, and after he won the election in Destiny, we figured we'd never see her again. I wish you could get an annulment from a parent." Tempe had felt like that once upon a time.

She turned toward the house to see how the work was going. The window was in and Freddie and the other guy were on either side of it on ladders securing it and putting up the trim. She couldn't help but be impressed.

"I was wondering," Jordie's quiet voice drew Tempe's attention back to the teen. "Do you think I'll end up… I mean, do you think I'm going to be… crazy, like her?"

"Ze—shootfire, Jordie, what kind of question is that?" Tempe asked.

"Well, you know how illness runs in families and with my mother being, well, you know… the way she is… I just thought, maybe it's hereditary."

"Not going to happen, Sweetheart."

Who was she to talk about family history? She thought about Phoebe and Dutch.

"All I can tell you is what I see—a beautiful, smart, intelligent young woman," *who deserved better than she got in the motherhood department.* "Normal in every way." *Except for the deremelei, but we're not going there right now.*

"Someone reminded me recently that families can offer some of the most challenging moments of our lives. Just because we're related by blood doesn't make the relationships work the way they do in the movies, or the way we expect." Taking one of Jordie's long fingered hands in hers, she said, "We can't pick our families. All we can do is supplement our lives with friends who provide what we're missing. They become family. That's what the SOAPS are to me, my sisters in every way but blood. They've mentioned including you in their ranks." Jordie smiled.

"And don't forget the *biggie*, you are the female spitting image of Jack Lang. Try not to be as hardheaded."

Jordie smiled. "He is that."

Tempe said, "So, absolutely, positively no. Get that thought right out of your head. You've never shown any signs of being strange, mean, or irresponsible."

Jordie nodded but there was something on her mind still. "You…"

Tempe waited patiently, fighting a shiver. Jordie asked, "You're not going to go away, are you? I mean you wouldn't stop seeing Daddy, stop being my friend because of *her*, would you?"

"Aww, baby, not on your life." Her question warmed Tempe. It was just what she needed. First the father had put voice to his feelings, and now his daughter. "I love you, Jordie. I couldn't want a little sister or friend to be any cooler than you."

Tears of relief spilled down Jordie's cheeks as she relaxed. "Thanks, Tempe. I love you, too."

Tempe hugged her and stroked her hair. "Why don't you go check on Shy, and I'll go get a jacket."

Freddie walked up to Tempe, "All done. The sky's getting darker. I'm going to get this machine back to Max and take Tommy home." His brows furrowed, "Are you sure you're feeling okay, Tempe?"

"Just a little chilled, Freddie, and kinda tired. It's been a busy two weeks."

"I'll say." What happened to *Youbetcha!* Tempe wondered.

"Thanks, again, Fred."

"It was the least I could do after breaking the other two, and you don't have to worry about this one. It's paid for." He held up his hand, "It's only right. Now, you just go on up to the living room and enjoy that view. Call me if you need anything." He slapped his gloves down in his palm and said, "Dave, load up."

Tempe stared. *Who was that man, and what did he do with my Freddie?*

# CHAPTER 25

JACK RECEIVED THE TEXT FROM MONTANA. IT CONVEYED enough urgency that he went directly from the gym to her house. He'd stopped by the gym to find Jordie working out her frustrations on the practice squad. Her friend, Jarell, had promised to stay close to her so he headed to Montana's.

He wanted to talk to the Dark Knight. He figured after what he'd seen earlier, the intensity in Flambé's expression, wherever Montana was, he'd find the warrior. There was something going on between them, or there would be if the Knight had his way. Montana's reaction at the ball proved she hadn't known what Flambé was before then, but they'd met in their supernatural forms, he'd bet on it—at the Bentsons' Saturday morning. The clues told him everything he needed to know.

Jack didn't care about the lady's missing abuser, or who had been responsible. He'd become imminently practical in the last few days. All he wanted to know was who was going to be on his side when all Chaos broke out. If Conor really was a forty-foot tall fire-breathing dragon, Jack wanted to recruit him for his team. He didn't know if that would be necessary, and if it was, he didn't have a clue what he could offer to gain the dragon's support.

HE DROVE INTO MONTANA'S YARD. THE SNOW COVERED grass looked as if something really large had wallowed around on it and there was no sign of any *thing* crawling away. *Uh-huh.* Jack got out and did a 360, searching for signs of a large scaly creature.

Montana walked toward him. She looked different. If he had to name it, he would probably say—radiant. *Female.* That wasn't it, she'd always looked female, just more of one than most, probably part of what made her Dinnshencha intimidating. But she'd said her powers were about gone, was this the vampire side? Had it gotten stronger? He willed himself not to step back as she approached, and smiled. Yep, radiant, glowing, and if anything, more confident.

"You rang?" He went for humor in case she was feeling a bit edgy. She didn't *look* edgy. She looked relaxed. If he didn't know bet—ah, that's what it was. She looked like a woman who had recently been, well… he settled on *satisfied.* Feeling the hairs rise between his shoulder blades, he searched the tree line once again. He found Montana's sword standing against a big stump near the edge of the woods.

The ground suddenly rocked under his feet and her sword toppled. Jack heard tree limbs breaking and a thunderous boom. He searched the sky, which was blacked out. He gulped, getting ready to run but the dragon's foot came down, brushing Jack's shoulder with its claws. A second massive appendage set down gently in comparison, and Jack backed away as he studied the black scales in front of him. His gaze traveled up, past the fiery red-rimmed belly, over powerful haunches, to wings that matched the creature's height.

It—he—stood patiently, looking down at Jack while he examined the powerful chest, the long thick neck and horned head. The scales that covered every square inch were like overlapping odd-shaped discs in an intricate pattern of red-trimmed ebony.

Jack looked into intelligent orange eyes, and watched as the nostrils flared and jaws opened. He should be afraid. That would have been smarter than his immediate reaction—awe. There was humor in the dragon's eyes as Jack put his hand out tentatively to touch one of the scales.

Three things happened at once: those giant talons dug into the grass in front of Jack, the massive wings lifted out and up, dragged the air out from under and around him like the intake on an F-18. He ducked. Then with a *whump*, they descended sharply, the claws rolling up like wheels under an airplane belly as several tons of dragon lifted into the air. The wings reached from one side of the wide clearing into the trees on the other.

Jack knew well the theory of flight, having studied aeronautics in the Navy. He understood the principles of thrust, drag, lift and weight when it came to aircraft. Was dragon flight the same?

He looked up at the belly of the massive beast, but it was too dark to make out details. It had obscured the sky like some great Battle star from an enemy galaxy. *Righteous!* As it rose and his vision adjusted he looked more closely at the scales on the underside of its body. They were shiny, and thicker than the ones he'd seen on the upper side of the legs and wings, the edges reflecting like mirrors. Like a stealth fighter, they probably made him invisible from below.

As he rose to get closer before the dragon took off, he realized it was virtually floating above him, pulsating on some magical current, or maybe it had some way of creating gas on the inside so it could float like a dirigible. He was transfixed, wanting to know everything about this flying miracle of magic or nature. He couldn't remember feeling compelled like this since he'd first been fascinated with flying.

It didn't look like the dragon was planning on going anywhere, just putting on an exhibition. That being the case, he should get out of the way before it landed and crushed him. Jack's lip quirked up in a smile. *You have a helluva BIG BAD persona, Flambé. Things were looking up.* He looked over at Montana and grinned, "Put a leash on that sucker and call him mine."

He jumped back as a roar of outrage, or at least rage,

rent the formerly snow-muffled afternoon, followed by the sound of snow-laden limbs each dumping their soggy load as the vibrations went through the trees. Before the sound died, the dragon, outlined in sparkles like sunlight on water, disappeared.

"What—" Jack spun around and found Conor standing within arm's reach. Flambé had transformed from a flying twenty-ton bird with claws, teeth and fire into his Knight form, complete with armor and swords.

"How do you do that?" Jack asked incredulously. Then kicked himself, but if anyone had ever told him he'd meet *Godzilla*... yeah, forget that. He hoped there were no bigger, scarier, more dangerous creatures than this out there, but somehow he figured there were. Hell, why would there be a need for a good POP this big, unless there were bad ones working for the enemy. It made sense.

"A leash?" Flambé glared at Jack, his eyes doing a weird swirly thing. "This is not *How to Train your Dragon.*"

"Right, okay, I'm duly impressed. Actually, I'm glad to find you here, Flambé. I see you've been... resting. Out here in the open," he hinted, pointing to the large area where the grass was torn up and mixed with snow and mud. "Were you by any chance at a certain household on the South side of town Saturday morning, the scene of a domestic abuse call?"

Conor looked at Montana who shrugged. Jack said, "That's what I thought."

Sword in hand now, Montana said, "Jack, Conor was just showing me a few moves. You might consider letting him work with you as well." Jack's gaze shifted to Conor. The Knight nodded but his expression didn't change.

Jack blurted, "You could have at least shown me a little fire," not believing he was standing there whining to a dragon that he wanted him to breathe fire. He had seriously flipped, but his eyes widened, and he figured he had a stupid grin on his face when Conor's nostrils drizzled fire briefly and those pupils flared like someone had stoked the fire behind a grate. "Yeah, uh, thanks." He rubbed his hands together, "So, Montana, I got a text from you—something about a confrontation with Tempe. Why didn't you mention it this morning?"

"When Tempe was here, I didn't want to bring it up in front of her. She doesn't have as much control as older Paramortals do. And then I got distracted…" they both knew by whom. "The important thing is that it shouldn't have happened. Paramortals shouldn't be able to go off on each other, even if the bond goes away, there's still the Oath. I thought we might ask Aurora about it." She tilted her head, and looked at Conor, "Do you know?"

"I've seen my share of Para-moons. What you are experiencing is the nullifying of the Oath when the Paramortal power is lost. I'm afraid there are many aspects to this event. There will be some who lose not only their power, but their will to stand for good. Defenders will refuse to defend and turn into predators, brother against brother, not just enemies, but good beings will act out of character, those who are simply moon-sick, for lack of a better term."

"Which is why it's called Chaos," Jack muttered. "And why Tempe and Aurora look so ill."

"I will be here, Lang. I have been—what did you call it, Branislava—tweaking her fighting standards, since she will'nae have her Dinnshencha power. You are a warrior, Lang. I would train you as well, tonight."

"I've never picked up a sword—"

Conor merely laughed, "*Ach*, nae. Merely how to use your hands and whatever you have to hand in fatal combat. Tonight."

"What about Dylan?" Jack asked.

Conor said, "Dylan's not going to be as much help as we'd like, eh?"

Montana said, "Dylan's personality is in retrograde."

"I've noticed," said Jack.

"It's all part of Chaos, little dragon. Every aspect of a being's life can be affected—personality, power, morality, physicality, and each being differently. There's no guarantee everyone will make it."

Jack ran his hands through his hair. "I'll be in touch, after I see how Tempe's faring." He hesitated, then turned back to Conor thinking about how Tempe and Aurora had looked when he'd seen them last. "A person can't just go retrograde like that and die, can they? You know… with moon-sickness?"

Montana looked at Conor worriedly. Conor didn't answer right away, but his empathetic expression told Jack all he needed to know. "Let's not worry about the wagon's path before the ox is tethered."

Montana muttered, "You mean, get the cart before the horse."

"He understands," said Conor.

Jack nodded gravely and hurried to his car, a sense of urgency gripping him.

# CHAPTER 26

AFTER JORDIE AND SHY DROVE AWAY TEMPE LOOKED AT the house. She should go in, get some warmer clothes on, but she didn't want to go inside. Out here she felt closer to the elements—air, water, and wind—though they were normally inside her. That's probably why she felt so… tired.

She scanned the dark sky, held her hand out to allow some of her Precipitaerie cousins, the snow skyers to land on her hand. She listened to their laughter and delighted in their bright reflections as they floated to earth. They were water elementals, the same little guys she'd seen sliding down Jack's pecs the morning they'd met. There were gazillions of them, so tiny as to be invisible until they latched onto each other and flowed as moisture or did their little sky-flying thing, competing against each other to create the largest and most intricate snowflakes. It's why you never found too alike.

She glanced at the *Forge*. The swamp was the reason Paramortals stayed so close to Destiny. The super pulse of power that ran through the bayou had a health spa like effect on them. Maybe the Forge, with its special rejuvenating qualities, would boost her energy. It was worth a try.

She strolled quickly to the bank. A short woman walked toward her, dressed in black pants and a lightweight cotton vest. She was from some South American indigenous tribe, with dark eyes, her hair a thick black braid, her body wide but spare. Her vest appeared to be designed merely for modesty as most of her chest, torso and arms were bare and painted with bright tattoos like the drawings of a first grader. As she got closer Tempe saw they were all different shapes, designs, and colors of snakes, some showing fang, some with wide circular yellow eyes, some outlined in bolder red or black. A few might have been just worms.

The woman's mouth widened in a smile displaying large straight teeth. Her flat cheeks didn't change shape, and her eyes never caught on to the greeting. Tempe nodded back. The woman had just come even with Tempe when the same eerie screeching roar she'd heard that morning with Dylan went up from the swamp. Tempe and the woman jumped. She gripped Tempe's hands, but both of them jerked back when a sharp prick like the shock of static electricity connected their fingers briefly.

The woman said, "Me disculpo". *I apologize.* Tempe looked the woman over. She backed away muttering and nodding, then her eyes went wide and she pointed over Tempe's shoulder.

Tempe spun around and watched as a figure crawled to the edge of the swamp and straightened on the bank, smoothing *her* hair, Tempe thought, primping. She was naked to the waist, her hair a bright yellow gold, and had eyes of blazing chartreuse green, like cheap stones from Party City. Those eyes seemed to be searching for something in particular, evidently not Tempe or the Indian woman, probably a man to entice. Her feet weren't visible so Tempe wondered if she might be Fae. She wasn't human; she was much too odd looking, and besides Fae loved running around in the nude, even in frigid weather. She turned to speak to the *snake* woman, to ask what she knew, why she was here, but she was gone.

Tempe's fingertip, the one with her *deremelei*, burned where she and the woman had touched. She held it up in the meager light of the snowy sky and spotted two tiny marks in the center of her living tattoo. She rubbed it with her fingers and licked it to take the sting away.

Her mind was fuzzy. "Lass, what's the matter?"

Tempe blinked, still rubbing at the sting on her fingertip. She'd intended to walk back to the house but had gotten only halfway up the hill when she'd stopped to admire the drifting snow.

"Tempe." Marty's voice. She blinked. Yes, *sweet little Marty*.

"I saw you with the demon, Tempest. Did she touch you? Attack you?"

Tempe looked down at her fingertip, then held it out to Marty. His head tilted as he studied the marks. "I've heard of them. The Naga. I think she's infected you. Let's go inside."

Tempe saw Jack's cruiser drive onto the grass by the house and said softly, "Jack."

"I'll find out what I can, Tempe," Marty said quickly and disappeared.

TEMPE NO LONGER FELT THE COLD GROUND BENEATH her. She looked wide-eyed at her first Para-moon. The huge transparent lavender disk was minutes from eclipsing Luna, with its pale white face edging closer to the great orb of Cache.

The stars were brilliant against an impossibly midnight blue sky on a windless, soundless night. Soundless, but for the joyous screams of the Precipitaerie, as they were expelled from the few remaining clouds.

As she bathed in the moons' rays, she listened to their chatter while they floated to earth, some in clusters, hanging on to each other like tandem parachutists, others solitary, all of them sparkling. They laughed, sighed, and screamed with delighted terror on their roller coaster ride to the earth below. They did ice like no one else.

She held her hand palm up, allowing the mini tandem teams to bulls-eye on her lifeline. "Tempe, you're cool, lass." She laughed. The air felt warm against her skin, as it became a frigid landing zone for hundreds of snow skyers.

The little tandem captain did a back flip on her palm bumping into other skyers as thousands more landed, then jumped or dived from her hands to catch air currents to the ground. She looked up and saw spin-drifts, spirals, and a blast of snow zephyrs racing the others, riding star-lighted threads of crystal and silver rays.

In that moment, every atom of her Tempestaerie heritage longed to jump into the fray. Precipitaerie continued to drift down landing on her arms, shoulders, and hair, reaching for their friends as they hooked up and created a layer of white crystals.

But as the sky filled with Cache's larger skyprint, her cousins quieted, drifting silently, floating at first, then… dropping from the sky like tiny white bowling balls. Straight to their deaths. A few called out to her for help, but she wasn't able to save them. She had nothing. *Menori* was gone.

As tears froze on her cheeks, their cries for help became less and less frequent. Finally, they went silent. Having neither the bulk nor the more intricate structure to withstand their loss of power, they'd simply died, coming to rest on Tempe's skin like a frozen wasteland, a snowflake graveyard.

As Jack turned down the street to Harmony, Jordie called to tell him she and Jarell had seen Tempe. His daughter was safely ensconced in the Lang mansion with Beffie stalking the halls while she watched the basketball games on TV with Jarell. She confirmed what Jack already knew—Tempe looked ill.

He saw Tempe as soon as he topped the hill. She was sitting on the ground looking up at that huge trouble-maker of an eclipse. He ran toward her, at first wondering if he should disturb her, if she was in some kind of Paramortal trance. But she looked so… lost. Her hair was nearly black, and she was covered in a light layer of frost.

Her palm was lifted to the sky, and on it was a layer of snow that had melted and frozen into a hard pack. Her gaze turned up toward Jack and his heart stumbled. On her cheeks he saw two ice crusted tear tracks. A shiver racked her. That jolted him into action. Her body temperature must be past critical because the snow was clinging to her skin, having formed a half inch deep layer on her shoulders.

Tempe had talked about her inner weather system and the fact that she was never cold. Ever. So this was no

Paramortal trance. Her power was completely gone, and Tempe was freezing to death.

More tears leaked from her eyes but they froze on her lower lids as she held her hand out toward Jack. "They're all dead."

*Who's dead?* He was suddenly terrified. He quickly shrugged out of his coat. "Here, Sweetheart, let's get you warmed up and get inside." He draped it around her, gave up trying to get her to stand and lifted her into his arms.

Before he'd seen her storms and witnessed her power, he'd thought her the feistiest woman he'd ever known. None of that was in evidence now. Any second, he feared, she'd be no more than an illusive dream, a memory, a ghost. "Hang in there for me, baby, please." He brushed her cold skin with his lips and closed his eyes, praying.

"I love you," he whispered, his voice raw.

Her eyes turned soft and she smiled up at him. "I've never loved anyone like I love you, Jack." Then her head fell against his shoulder, and he realized he couldn't see her breath.

Jack was gripped with a new urgency. Before long, it was going to be like a National Conference for bad guys, without many of the Paramortals to help contain it. Jack would be the Commander of an odd assortment of merry men and women.

Destiny had turned out to be more like Middle Earth than the Mayberry he'd hoped for. And his new friends were probably hoping he'd turn out to be less like an ex-Navy pilot and more like Aragorn.

Conor had said it would be friend against friend, brother against brother, some with power, others without; some evil and some just plain sick. How would he tell the difference? All he knew was that for the woman in his arms, he would fight; and for the people in Destiny and beyond. By God or Zeus, or whoever was controlling the Para-moon, his side was going to win.

A large cloud must have passed in front of the moon and Jack looked up. But there against the backdrop of the giant lavender disc was the silhouette of the dragon, and on his back stood a woman riding him like some kind of mythological barrel racer, her sword lifted to the sky.

He experienced a flash of hope, accepted the enemy's challenge and shouted, "Hooyah!"

GRAB THE NEXT PARAMORTALS BOOK, BLAME IT ON the Moon

**But before you go. . .**

To find out **how to claim your free** signed reader-exclusive mystery gift email liviaquinn@liviaquinn.com

Don't forget to sign up for Livia's spam-free newsletter. Subscribers will receive exclusive offers, news about new books release and access to special giveaways.
Click here to sign up http://bit.ly/2lJhOB5

*For more information:*
www.liviaquinn.com
liviaquinn@liviaquinn.com

Facebook Twitter Instagram Amazon Bookbub

READ AN EXCERPT OF BLAME IT ON THE MOON

*JACK*

*Don't stand in front of a dragon. This is not rocket science.*

The gravel surface crunched under the cruiser's tires as I

pulled up next to Ryan's vehicle. At first I didn't see my friend and deputy. Then silhouetted against the moon a rifle barrel, dark and steady, stuck out from behind the roof of the deputy's car.

I followed the direction of the rifle. I hadn't noticed because the lake had been eerily silent, as if it was just another calm winter night, the quiet not preparing me for the sight in front of me.

Surrounded by water five hundred yards from the bank was a bass boat, one of those fancy high end models the pros outfitted themselves with. And circling above him like buzzards waiting for their prey to die, were hundreds of... well, the fisherman had told Ryan they looked like pterodactyls and I had to agree. He'd lowered himself into the boat as one by one the gangly looking things dove down to snap at him, as if toying with him before going in for the kill. The only thing visible against the moonlit water was the motor and the man's head, which occasionally popped up above the side. He was flattened onto the raised platform of the boat in a effort to minimize what they could snatch.

When Ryan spoke, low and serious, I knew his days of escape or denial were over. "What the hell are those things? Is it... too late to pretend I'm not in Kansas?"

Ryan's words may have been light but his body language said he wasn't fooled. He expected the whole truth. It was hard to tell how big the things were but there was no trouble grasping their deadliness.

"I'm sorry, Ryan. What you're seeing is real. I estimated there were over two hundred 'birds' in the sky, silently circling the bass fisherman like carrion sniffing impending death. But they so obviously weren't birds; they didn't squawk or make any other bird sounds which would alert their prey.

The flap of wings overhead preceded one of the creatures landing on the ground between us. It wasn't moving. When it hit the ground I realized how much the distance distorted the size and weight of the things. This one was well over three hundred pounds and probably could have eaten me and Ryan both. Ryan jumped back and shot it several times, though the bullets didn't seem to penetrate far into the tough hide.

I said, "Just don't shoot the biggest one. He's on our side."

One of the flock dove toward the man in the boat and was within striking distance when light on the water dimmed like a cloud obscuring the moon. The great body of the black dragon, wings expanded, glided into the center of the flock, releasing short bursts of fire, immediately searing the devils into clunky carcasses with gravity doing the rest.

They fell out of the sky making loud splashes around the boat as they cannonballed into the water. Like an F18 doing a flyby of the control tower, Conor's giant wings tucked. He performed two perfect barrel rolls and hurtled toward us. The sight of his brilliant blazing eyes and flared nostrils, not to mention the wide mouth filled with thousands of sharp teeth produced a strangled warble from Ryan before he hit the gravel. *Overkill, Conor.* I thought he'd fainted until I heard him holler, "Duck."

"No, that's a dragon, my man." A chuckle rose from my chest as I stood my ground.

I couldn't explain why I wasn't scared but every time I observed Conor's dragon form I felt... I felt *envious.* Besides Flambé was a knight and he seemed to be testing me. Maybe Conor recognized a fellow warrior with a love of flying and understood my appreciation of his abilities.

"Jack! What the hell was that? Ryan scrambled to his feet and stared as Conor soared back into the sky and aimed for the rest of the flock. "It... nah," Ryan put the back of his hand to his forehead. "I must be hallucinating. Damned if that..."

A laugh burst out before I could contain it. Ryan might as well experience a bit of the giant reality slope I'd had to climb if he was going to adjust quickly.

"Ah, shit. You're just standing there like we didn't just see a big ass fire-breathing dragon swoop down out of the sky and..."

"Well what did you think you were aiming at, Big Black Bird?"

His shoulders dropped and he stared at me. "Jack, there's no such thing as dragons." This was met by a roar from the sky and a belch of flame so large it reflected on the water below as Conor took out twenty of the demons at once.

"A month ago, I would have said the same, Ryan. And that went for Faeries, and Dinnshenchas, and vampires, genies, and weather witches."

Ryan's mouth was open as he absorbed my meaning. Clamping it shut he rammed his hand through his hair. He was completely missing the show in the sky above him. I watched and Ryan said, "What are... you telling me there's... I mean, did you say...vampires?"

Order Blame it on the Moon here

### Veterans Resources

***Please Support our troops!*** It's not a cliché that we owe our veterans our very freedom. Many of our soldiers return with Post Traumatic Stress Syndrome (PTSD), Traumatic Brain Injury (TBI), debilitating injuries and illnesses. Trauma affects the *whole family*.

**Veterans Crisis Line** call 800-273-8255, press #1
**Urgent**: Vet needing shelter? Call 1(877) 4AID-VET
**Suicide:** If you or a loved one has contemplated suicide, call or go online to:
http://www.stopsoldiersuicide.org
**Women Veterans Health**
**Drug Rehab** addiction help https://drugrehab.com
**Mesothelioma** Mesothelioma Navy "Most veterans suffering from a service-related asbestos disease never bother to file a VA Disability Compensation and/or Pension Claim; either because they don't think they are eligible, or simply assume the VA will deny them. "
**Volunteer or Donate to help a vet**
**American Legion** (help applying for benefits)
**Vet to Vet assistance** (a fellow vet helps you w/ info)
https://nvf.org/veterans-request-assistance/

SEE MORE ON MY WEBSITE LIVIAQUINN.COM